GOD'S GATE

And Polecat Tom

by

G.H. White

PREFACE:

There are more questions buried in the earth than there are answers. Scientists say the earth is 4 billion years old, the star we circle some 5 billion years, while our Milky Way galaxy is around 14 billion years. Sumerian writing is some 5000 years old. Yet, according to the Bible our species has only been around some 6000 years. Given the Bible is the most sold book in print, how can we justify the differences?

The following Science Fiction work is one attempt at justification.

CONTENTS

1-THE ROAD

As the Arizona sunshine bore down on the cracked asphalt of Interstate 10, truck tires sizzled in whiney protest of the weight they bore at speed.

The same sun bore down intensely on a lone traveler as his long arms scissored rhythmically pulling his thin, emaciated body behind. Few passing motorists would pay attention to this traveler.

This highway he walked on passed through Joshua Tree National Park, connecting California, Arizona, and points West to East in a black ribbon of auto and truck passage.

Joshua Tree Park had its own surreal draw that claimed the imagination of many travelers through the centuries humankind had been here. If these trees were sentient, they would likely have little patience for the human lives so short in comparison, as Joshua Trees need 50 years to mature and can live up to 500 years.

Early Mormon settlers noted the up-reaching tree's branches reminded them of Joshua reaching for God.

Hence, Joshua Tree!

At times, Interstate 10 would appear as an escape route for those attempting to leave the Los Angeles basin, allowing flight at highway speeds Eastward.

The traffic East predictably increased after earthquakes but had sped up in later years because of overburdening taxation and increasing social issues. In the last decade, it had become infamous for more people leaving the state than moving in. A most significant time in California's population history and contradictory to the Horace Greely chant, "Go West Young Man."

Our traveler likely did not know that in the relatively distant past, courageous adventurers had come into the area for gold and other minerals to make their fortune. Many died in the process.

When the film industry began to develop, in the early 1900s, hordes had moved to California seeking the riches, freedom, and stardom of many would-be cinema stars. Most found shattered dreams instead. And, many died.

Indeed, some lives were in partial ruin in the present, as the cars headed away from California.

Such an escapee was Reverend Bill, the hitchhiker missing a car. He used the oldest human transportation method. The one that allowed our very distant cousins to leave Africa and spread out to the rest of the world.

Bill used his feet!

2-REVEREND BILL

A passing motorist would think it common to see a hitch-hiker with his thumb stuck out. But Reverend Bill was unique when compared to any other highway traveler.

Drivers might have seen his shoulder-length, dirty blond hair, and his six-foot-two-inch frame. Perhaps, they might have noticed his backpack. They would not know that inside he had few survival items, like a Swiss Army knife, a few changes of socks and underwear, a worn bedroll tied with rope and little else.

Though they could guess, they would not know he was a broken man, without a home, a family, or any direction in life. Only this road gave him a purpose for his immediate future.

These passing motorists certainly would not know this broken man was hugely successful and rich in his younger years.

During his travels, whenever he could, he would wash himself and his clothes, frequently letting both dry as he walked along trying to catch his next ride.

Today, Bill's gray eyes scanned the horizon for storm clouds. Though rains were unusual in the Mohave Desert, sudden flooding could take place during one. Time might be needed to seek higher ground.

Just last week he had narrowly missed a gully washer, sweeping him suddenly awake and downstream, in thigh-deep water. Luckily, he had slept lying uphill in the gully, so he did get a chance to wake and breathe prior to being swept away. He vowed he would be more careful in the future.

Bill's eyes had a piercing quality that commanded anyone's attention if they looked at him closely. This was balanced with a gentle shy smile that softened that piercing gaze.

He had been an Evangelical child prodigy! From his childhood's elevated stage, he had preached the eternal love of God and Jesus as a mature man would. He knew virtually the entire King James Bible and could quote one verse after another, jumping from Book to Book like an ice skater's feet propelling a person along the ice.

He would scream out to a packed congregation, "Do you know Jesus? Do you want his love?"

Hundreds of thousands of people came to hear this child of God speak over the years, and the money flowed in.

His Revival Tent would fill to capacity in almost any city, from Los Angeles to Seattle Washington, to New York and Washington D.C. and points in between. His caravan of buses was always ready to load up and find the next city of suffers.

By the time his 40+ singers would begin to sing the praises of the Lord, people were eagerly awaiting the passing of the plate so they could put their money into the offering.

He loved the masses--he loved their power.

He felt this energy was fed into his soul, and he, in turn, tried to re-direct it to the heavens, to get God's attention. He believed he could personally help everyone find their pathway to God.

The youngster, Reverend Bill would lash out, "You must be saved! You must accept Jesus!"

His congregations believed that he could heal. Most times, he believed he could as well.

His ailing father desperately wanted to believe in these powers as their lives depended on the money that came into the plate.

Bill's father, Franklin D. Fogarty, secretly mourned he was the only family Bill had left. Both, he and Dora were only children, born to mothers later in years. As the two of them grew up, their respective parents withered and died in different ways. Franklin was trained as a business analyst and for much of his life, he provided very well for Dora and Bill. Dora liked to play the piano and was quite good, as she had had offers to attend a few universities. She never accepted, as she really did not like to study.

Franklin spent two decades building his client list, but a few bad business decisions and one of his clients decided to sue him out of existence.

Now broke, making ends meet by working at the local hardware store, Franklin and Dora had William. And, though they were proud of him, it was so difficult to pay the bills.

A few years passed and Dora was pregnant again. Dora, died while attempting to give birth to their second child when Bill was only four. The medical staff believed it was related to Preeclampsia, but Dora's organs started shutting down so quickly, they were unsure.

Not only did Franklin lose his precious wife, but also his second child they had hoped was a girl. Though they never expected their son to become something bigger than life, they certainly hoped their daughter would live to balance their family and future dreams.

His father, drowning in grief, could only follow a path that lay before him, as he had lost any strength to change his future. So, as young Bill paved the way, Franklin followed and supported him as best he could. At least, he could use his business knowledge to help his son.

Bill's "visions" began during that time frame just after his mother died.

Bill's visions told him what he must do, what he must learn. The visions spoke of destinations, sermons, how to hold himself, how to project the Word with his very body. Sometimes, they came when he was asleep and dreaming, sometimes he was awake. But they came frequently. He began to dream of the Bible, and how he would gather and guide an audience of many people.

Though his father doubted the veracity of the visions, he slowly began to see a future for Bill and himself.

The blind came to the Revival tents so Bill could help them see. The deaf came, to hear again. Most pitiful of all were the ones without hope, who were desperate to find any help in this world. Indeed, the hopeless came to the one place where hope was on full display for them.

Reverend Bill embodied hope. It seemed the world was drowning in tears needing a Reverend Bill for a future without fear. It was his mission, to lay hands upon and feel the healing heat of Jesus flow through his hands. It was his mission to give them a reason to carry on with their lives and to stop their despair.

As time progressed, and this child became a teenager, his voice began to change.

A voice that had once sounded authoritative and strident, full of confidence. His voice had been a high horn, singing God's Words.

Puberty caused it to become an irritating sound, likened to fingernails scratching up and down the spine of the listener. His childlike looks became elongated, almost comical in appearance. As his bones stretched, he lost his smooth stride, and became curious in his movements, almost halting between steps.

Just like any other young man is tormented when puberty rages, young Bill was afflicted as well, with nightly visits from the lust demon. Some of his dreams involved young and mature ladies from his Revival Tents.

Bill was embarrassed and frustrated that his body seemed to ignore his Godly intentions.

"What caused this?" he asked. "Have I not prayed hard enough?" He asked for forgiveness from this rebellion of his flesh and his dreams.

Had he not preached directly against this as a sin?

"Let not thy seed, fall to the ground."

His failing confidence in himself and his own faith began to show in his performances. His tours brought in less and less tithing. Less money caused more pressure. Increased pressure caused less confidence, which caused less 'healing', which caused less tithing. A cycle of failure began for Reverend Bill and seemed to accelerate to the point where his audience noted it as well.

Bill's 'healing' powers seemingly disappeared and that, too, caused less interest from his passionate public. The money flowed out. His father died the year after his ministry ended, bankrupt, with many creditors demanding to be paid, which was followed by lawsuits.

He was now neither a child nor a prodigy having lost his faith and himself sometime in the past. William 'Reverend Bill' Fogarty, was a 'has-been' at the young age of fifteen!

In his heart, he knew God had not left him, but he had left God.

He had generated more money in six years than many people earn in their entire lives. But his golden run was over. The lawsuits took everything.

Because of his traveling lifestyle, Reverend Bill's public education had been minimal. As a result, he was not prepared to finish high school and was certainly not equipped for college.

But, his education on the road was invaluable as he could escape his past and walk towards the future. He knew to go to the main road, stick his thumb out, and wait for a trucker, friendly farmer, or older couple to stop and pick him up.

Sometimes, the people who picked him up would give him a little food and water. But if not, he knew to look in garbage bins behind cafes, or in the national park areas in their garbage bins.

In this way, he moved from city to city meeting new souls. He learned more from everyone he met.

Out of old habit, at first, he tried to convert these poor people with the Word of God. Slowly, it dawned on him, many travelers did not appreciate his efforts, as he sometimes got an "AMEN", but usually a very short tense ride down the road.

3-WATERING HOLE-QUARTZITE

After several hitches on Interstate 10, Bill was now surrounded by Arizona desert and scrub brush.

He was just outside the touristy frontier town of Quartzsite, Arizona, which could be the Recreational Vehicle capital of the world; a destination he had achieved the day before.

Most of the businesses in town had huge parking lots meant for the RVs. Quartzsite sits at the present-day intersection of I-10 and Route 95. Quartzsite itself is a hot and dry city, with temperatures as high as 120 degrees F. and less than 4 inches of rain annually.

Bill would never know that it was established in the 1860s as a waterhole for stagecoaches along dirt paths leading to forts and mines in Arizona and points westward. Weary travelers and horses needed rest, food, and water found all here in Quartzsite.

Bill would have likely hitched over the nearby Colorado River but was certainly ignorant of the fact that he was also near the Colorado Indian Reservation that had tribes like the Utes, Pai, and Hualapai. The Indian tribes were forced here in 1874 via a peace treaty. Years of conflicts with soldiers from Fort Mojave and local miners searching for gold caused this action.

For Bill and others, a desert area implied the lack of water and plant life, but oddly enough, there were widely scattered waterholes which attracted various birds like, Doves, Woodpecker, Hummingbirds, Blue Heron, small Hawks, and so on. By the same reasoning, people would believe there to be a lack of plant life, but there is a wide variety of hardy plant life throughout the area such as the Western Yarrow, Teddy-bear Cholla, Spruce-top Grama, the Walking-stick Cactus, and Burr-Ragweed, are only a few. The Kofa National Wildlife is in this area, protecting the Desert Bighorn Sheep, and providing refuge for Badgers, Foxes, and more.

The most important fact for Bill he would learn was the Hualapai and Hopi Indians had myths about this area. These myths included strange people coming and going, armed with great knowledge, interacting with the local Indians.

There are many Petroglyphs or rock reliefs located in this part of the country. Some of the most amazing are near Theba Arizona, in the Painted Rock area, bordered by the Gila River. Painted Rock has some 800 strange images. Across the American Southwest, one can find Petroglyph images of deer, coyotes, and other creatures. However, there are also images of creatures with spindly bodies, huge eyes, and large heads, sometimes with antennae. The Indian legends describe how the "Star People" or "Ant People" helped mankind survive through various world-ending catastrophes.

Reverend Bill did not know any of this, though parts of it would become important to his future.

Last night, he had slept behind a truck stop, next to a refrigeration unit. Its exhaust heat kept him moderately warm and its hum helped block out the vehicles coming and going through the cold desert night.

This morning, Bill awoke to a bright, cloudless sunrise, with chirping birds. They sounded so happy, while he felt so sad.

He got up, stretched, yawned, looked around, and relieved himself against a Saguaro cactus that loomed over his head.

Then, he walked to the main road and warmed up his thumb. The day wore on. No-one stopped for him, though many passed. Their speeding vehicles caused hot winds to blow trash against his legs and dust into his eyes.

He would stop whenever a car was coming so that he could stick his thumb out in that special way that meant, 'Give Me a Ride, please.'

Just to break the monotony, Bill kept walking East on I-10.

4 - TRUCKING
WITH POLECAT

The Sun was almost over his head when a rust bucket of a truck pulled over to stop slightly ahead of Bill. In violent protests, its brakes squealed to the world. A tire grabbed and left a black mark thirty feet long, while the other tires still turned.

While the truck sat waiting on him to catch up to it, Bill saw black smoke coming from underneath its body. The truck wheezed, sputtered and trembled as a dying man wracked with his last cough.

The body of the truck must have been red at one time, though now the appearance was closer to a molted brown. Reverend Bill could see one tire with no tread; the others appeared to have little more.

As he walked closer to the truck, he glanced in the bed. He saw a tire jack, claw hammers, paintbrushes, two spare tires, a paper sack, and a well-worn, grave digger shovel.

"A working man?" he asked himself, "What is that smell? "

The closer he got to the cab of the rust bucket-- the stronger the smell. This was not a pleasant smell; not like flowers or fresh-cut grass.

No, this was Man Smell at his worst.

"Howdy partner!" the driver said, cheerfully. "I guess you need a ride. Come on and hop in, sit with me. I haven't talked to a bloody soul in a week. I spent a lot of time out there!"

With his chin, he pointed to the desert hills.

He watched Bill look in the chinned direction, and said, "Nah, no use looking, there is nothing there. So, what you waiting for, a fancy invite? Jump in or stand back. I ain't got much to do, but I ain't got no time to waste either!" the driver stated.

Bill surreptitiously audited his driver.

Bill thought to himself, "Yeah, a PoleCat! That's what he smells like," thinking of a skunk.

Still thinking to himself, Bill thought, "God, what a poor soul. Beard a foot long. UH, he must chew tobacco, if that's the brown stain running down his beard."

The driver's stomach was just above and spilling over his belt. He wore glasses, with one limb missing and the other heavily taped with masking tape, which barely hung from his large bulbous nose.

'PoleCat' wore an undershirt with indescribable stains on it. Bill believed that the shirt could tell what PoleCat had eaten for the last month. The smell only supported his suspicion.

As Bill got into the truck he asked, "Mind if I roll down my window to the bottom, and flip this vent towards me?"

The driver waved a hand, "Sure. The desert smells great. You will want that air coming at you!"

In Bill's mind, he knew the desert smell had to be better than the inside of the truck.

The driver pushed in the clutch to grab the first gear. But the grinding noise that came with this action made Bill question if the clutch worked.

Polecat hit the gas four or five times to coax the engine into a higher speed that might get the truck moving. Slowly, the clutch was let out, then pressed back in when the engine speed dipped suddenly.

Again, the gas pedal was feathered, until the engine speed climbed once more. Again, the grinding noises, more sputtering noises, again the gas was feathered, while the clutch was double pumped to move into second gear.

It coughed and bucked, but it continued to move, as the ground speed gradually climbed.

Finally, third gear.

Bill found himself willing the truck to go faster.

Polecat paid some attention to the road, as he continually had to correct the truck's path by swinging the steering wheel of the truck left and right to stay somewhat in his lane.

The driver said, "Been out in the Mohave a while. It gets too damn hot this time of year in the afternoon. I love it though!" he said, and then smiled through his beard.

" 'Specially when the cactus blooms. You know, every now and then, the rain will come in. Whatever I'm doing I stop and go watch the desert come alive. Things get real pretty and active, just after the rain. Prettiest little flowers come out, and all the sand critters act like they're full of pep. And, the Cactus? Well, partner, you would have to see it to believe it. I am very partial to the Saguaro, but the Hedgehog Cactus is mighty fine."

Polecat suddenly caught himself, rubbed his right hand on his T-shirt, and awkwardly poked it at Bill.

"Oh, excuse me. I don't see people enough to remember how I am suppost to act."

Bill shook his extended hand, while the truck wandered into the other lane.

"Most folks call me Nuts, but my real name is Tom." He looked slyly at Bill and gave him a wink, his beard moved in direct response.

Bill stared down the road to keep his composure, as the truck nose swung left and right, in a manner that could make a person feel like they were on a small boat in a big ocean. He concentrated instead on a desert view that seemingly had no end or beginning, with only the black asphalt ribbon to give it any definition.

Much of the roadside was mostly brown spreading to a red hue, with the occasional green cactus and roadside scrub brush. The few signs of life were vultures flying high overhead, lizards and other desert creatures on the ground. Once he thought he saw a dog, then realized it must have been a coyote.

A vision began in his head imagining what other people thought of Tom and his own overlapping image of a Polecat.

This soon became a humorous image in Bill's mind.

Bill's laugh was quiet and controlled at first. But then became louder, until it finally erupted as a 'belly laugh'.

"You wouldn't happen to like Polecats, would you Tom?" Reverend Bill asked. Bill felt like he might wet his pants.

5 –TOM

Tom looked at him in a quizzical way, and asked, "What in the world are you laughing at? My name? What is funny about a man's name?
" I know I talk funny ta folksies! I never had a formal education! But I ain't stupid! So there!" Tom finished with a flourish putting his eyes back on the road and snapping Sara back into the lane. "And, what in tarnation is a Polecat, sir?"

Bill couldn't reply while he was gasping for air. As he calmed down, he knew he had to correct himself. He just waved his hands as if to move the offense away.

Tom angrily said, "Alright, Mr. Smarty Pants, what's your handle?" His smile had disappeared replaced by a spreading red face.

Bill took several deep breaths, slowly gaining control and immediately, he felt embarrassed. Reverend Bill began, "Please accept my apology. I haven't had much food or water lately, and I might be just a little off in the head! Many in this country would say a Polecat is like a critter that lives off the land." He avoided his definition of Polecat smell.

That seemed to calm Tom down some, as he turned his glaring eyes back to the road, while his face lost some of the red hues.

Bill took a longer calming breath and said,

"William is my name! But everyone calls me Bill, and I'm very glad to meet you!"

"Of course, you are," Tom said with a smile that showed only as a slight uplift to the hair around where his lips should be.

He was watching Bill from the corner of his eyes. "You see I'm God, and I plan to turn your life around!"

Bill, of course, looked startled.

But he had stopped laughing at Tom.

Tom smiled just a little more and then burst out laughing. His belly shook, his beard waved, the top of his forehead became beet red, his cheeks took on a pinker color again.

"Man! You ought to see yourself. You look as if you had seen a ghost," Tom had clearly paid him back.

"So, where do you hail from? How is the United States doing? How is that new prez fellow doing these days, the one from Chicago with the funny last name? He reminds me of a used car salesman," he said while shaking his head. "Not the one that sold me this truck. No, that was an honest salesman. But I can't trust that Chicago fellow!"

"You know, way back I was a gunner, in the Marines. I shot at a few of the enemies, not sure if I hit anything. But I hope I at least made 'em dirty their diapers."

"Just in general, a man that smiles that way with such a silky voice is just liable to run off your wife and rape your dog! Listening to those Washington D.C. boys sometimes make me think I was shooting at the wrong enemy."

Bill was getting the idea, that silence was indeed rare around this man. But he found him entertaining, if not horribly dated.

He did manage to break in on Tom's flow for a short introduction. Bill said, "To your earlier question, I grew up in California, but later on traveled all over with my father." He decided to leave out his ministry and how successful it was.

"As to the United States, we seem to be doing pretty well on the business front, but there is more division between people than I can remember. It seems like everyone is fighting about something. And, you cannot trust what you read or hear, it seems from the news outlets. Two sides, stuck in their corners, refusing to listen to the other."

There was a new president beyond the "Chicago Fellow" that Bill decided to keep quiet about.

In his stunted travels, he had learned to avoid discussing politics, religion, or any number of social concerns. He never knew which sensitive button would cause the driver to pull over and ask him to put his flat feet on the ground.

He covered more miles by keeping his mouth shut.

6 - VANITY

Polecat droned on and Bill smiled.

As the ride progressed, and Tom spoke, Bill daydreamed what he might do in Arizona on a street corner, espousing his faith to a handful of folks while saving souls. He then imagined being in front of thousands of people once again, with their spiritual power pouring through him, and their love and adulation making him feel complete.

Bill pictured himself getting up on something like a park bench in a city or a wooden box. He would then sermonize on the Ten Commandments, Acts 2:38, Revelations, and try to scare the Bejesus out of as many as he could.

"Are you saved? Hellfire awaits you if you are not!" he said to himself.

He knew many would ignore him, others would scorn him, worse yet, were those that would shake their heads because they pitied him. In all his travels, since losing his confidence, he did not believe that he had saved one soul.

He caught himself.

As Lucifer had been cast out of Paradise for vanity, he had too. Pride goes before the fall, and he had fallen very far.

"I would like to save one more soul before I die!" He thought mournfully to himself.

The old man, Tom, had never stopped talking about his past. The places he had been. The children he had helped. The smile of his life was spread across his words.

Bill realized that Tom had no room for vanity, he just lived.

Bill came to understand that despite what Polecat Tom had said earlier about the 'immigrants and enemies' Tom hated no one.

He loved animals and people. He spoke lovingly of sparrows and rattlesnakes. He rambled on about flowers and the tall pines in the mountains. Of lost tourists, politicians, the guy that took his gas money from him in Tucson, where he had several American Indian friends.

Anyone that met him would probably call him 'Nuts', but in a loving way. Bill bet many looked forward to seeing old Tom if they had the time necessary to let him talk.

Tom spoke of his love for the deserts, the hills, even dirt. He jokingly made fun of his cleanliness, and simply explained the earth took a bath whenever it rained, and he was a Man of the Earth.

Here was a man out of touch with television, radio, newspapers, and telephones, but he enjoyed just being and living.

He even loved his old truck.

7 – SARA

"You like Sara?" Tom asked.

"Huh?" Bill asked.

"My truck! This is Sara! She's a little contrary, but she is faithful to me. Had her these fifty years. She's got a few miles on her, and you got 'a treat her easy, but she gets me all of this desert!" an obviously proud Tom said one hand spanning the horizon. "Oh, every now and then she breaks down and I have to find a part. And, of course, I must keep the brakes braking and the tires turning. But, all part of the plan."

Bill caught this last sentence and assumed if the truck rolled at all or stopped at all, Tom did nothing to it, since both brakes and tires were in horrible condition.

He began again, "Ain't far ahead I'll be turning off the main drag. Pity you're coming through here right now. This hill we are on is part of the Aquarius Mountains. 'Absolutely beautiful when the sun is going down."

" Ya want 'ta rack at my place? I've got room for ya. It would be a lot better than sleeping in the open? Or, I can drop ya on this highway when I turn off. So?" Tom waited for an answer.

Bill asked himself, "He seems to talk on the inhale and exhale. Does he ever breathe?"

Bill said, "I would be honored to stay in a house. It has been a very long time for me to be inside walls with a roof."

Tom exclaimed, "Great! There'd be no white men up there for years. Had a few bears, other critters, you know. I can offer ya a cot and breakfast!"

Tom paused, and then started again, "Tomorrow morning, we'll drive into Brenda Town. Not much to see there in a place so small, but I have got to get some supplies. You can decide your next steps from there!"

Within an hour, they had turned off the main road, south onto Gold Nugget Rd.

Sara, the truck, went quickly from good asphalt to a road badly needing repair. Another turn to the South and they were on loose gravel, and still climbing in altitude. Now a hard, hairpin right and they were on dirt, with the road pitching and bumping, while the occupants hung on as best they could.

The old truck sang, screamed, and squealed, but Sara clawed forward.

Tom talked through every turn and pothole.

Finally, Tom turned a curve, passing a huge rock on his left.

He pulled to a squealing stop and put Sara's emergency brake on. He then turned the engine off and jumped outside.

The truck began to roll backward as Tom likely knew it would.

Tom pulled a brick from behind his seat and placed it behind the wheel in the rear with no tread with it.

8 - TILLEY'S HOUSE

Tom said, "Well, here we are! Home!"

Bill, looked up from the truck and saw Tom's 'house.'

It was closer to a shack. At least one wall was not square. The tin roof looked as if the rust was the paint, with a few old tires thrown on to hold roof panels in place.

The front 'yard' was a potpourri of old axles, plows, wheels, etc. It looked as if snakes used it for seasonal snake conventions.

Tom said, "I built it myself!" As if that needed to be said.

A dog appeared, running and barking towards them. It appeared to weigh twenty or so pounds, had the long thin muzzle of a collie, and had the squarish head of another breed, with floppy ears. Some of its hair was short and shaggy. All of it was dirty, with strands of local vegetation as well as matted sand that surrounded the area obviously part of its coat.

"Perfect match for Tom," Bill said to himself.

It bound up to Tom, and ran around him like a demon, barking the whole time. He bent to pet it, but it wouldn't stay still long enough. He called it by name.

"Tilley! Sweetie Tilley! Good Girl!"

"Did you call it Tilley?" Bill asked.

"Yeah! That's short for Attila the Hun. Isn't she a terror?" Tom chuckled at his own joke. "She's a great dog though. Problem is, I can't keep any chickens 'round her."

Suddenly, Tilley leaped into Tom's arms and put her head on his shoulder, next to his neck. They nuzzled like this for a few short moments, then he put her down.

Tilley started circling them again while barking the entire route. Then she ran into something that looked like a weatherworn chicken coop, with no square corners, likely built by Tom.

Bill chuckled, as she peeped out the door and barked, once more, as if to say, "There! I made my statement! My home, my friend! You, stranger, are not welcome!"

Tom led him inside the 'house' and showed him a small cot.

"That would be yours!" Tom said. "The sun will be setting soon. You can stay up a while if you want to talk some more, or just hit the hay!"

Bill nodded, and said a quick thanks, but then promptly collapsed on the cot. The cot was likely hard to some, but to Bill, it was as soft as clouds.

He went quickly to sleep, without dreams, and obviously without moving, as the next morning, he woke in the same spot, with his spittle running down his chin.

Birds chirping, slowly woke him. It took several seconds to remember where he was.

He sat up on the edge of the bunk, swung his legs to the side. He stood stretching his arms overhead and slowly twisting them side to side. Then, he knelt at the cot side to perform his morning prayers.

Tom walked in and snorted.

Bill became irritated at the thought of Tom making fun of

his prayers.

"I am praying to my Maker. A little respect would be appreciated!" Reverend Bill stated.

Tom laughed, "You're right, of course. I apologize. But your knees are in dog poop. Didn't you smell it?"

Bill looked down, and for the first time noticed it. "Yeah, well I guess I was not awake, or my nose wasn't."

Tom said, "You have a morning gift from Tilley. She is telling you you don't belong!"

Tom continued, "But there is something appropriate about kneeling down in dog poop and going through a ritual of talking to someone who will never talk back. But, don't you mind me!" Polecat exclaimed, holding both hands out, palm up while turning away to the 'kitchen'.

"You might want to clean off those pants before breakfast, though. There's a small spring out da back. Don't turn North, go right out the door, and head straight away. It's a mite cold, but the dog poop will come off in the water with a bit of scrubbing and hitting the rocks with those pants," Tom said while walking away.

He suddenly turned back to face Bill and said, "You know? Water is kinda special! It doesn't care what you do with it. You can drink it, boil it to cook food, wash your butt with it, put it in any shape container and it will take that shape. A body can even get the dog poop off clothes in water. It don't care!" Both arms went up for emphasis.

'PoleCat Tom' looked at the ceiling, thoughtfully, and said, "A person's soul ought to be somewhat the same way. Always there, despite what people might say or do to you. A soul that flows like water. What do they say in the 'Good Book', if someone hits your cheek? Turn your mug and give him a shot at the other side!"

Tom was obviously proud of this diatribe.

"Curious, I never thought of that before." Reverend Bill remarked. But Tom did make sense, in a strange kind of way.

9 – DOG POOP

Bill wandered down to the small spring, took his denim trousers off, and proceeded to wash the dog poop off his knees. He decided to wash his shirt as well, then his body. The cold water quickly caused goosebumps and he hurried the washing process. He had his spring-washed jeans and shirt lying on the grass, where the sun could dry them out.

He saw Tilley on the spring bank, smelling around his clothes. She squatted, and made water on his clothes, all the while looking Bill straight in his eyes.

Bill yelled at her. "Tilley, come on. I just got them clean. Git! Git on out of here!"

She ambled casually off into the brush.

Tom came out of the shack, where he was preparing breakfast, and asked, "What in blue blazes is going on?"

"Attila the Hun just pissed on my washed clothes!" Bill screamed.

"Oh?" Tom chuckled.

With his right-hand pointing at Bill, while chuckling to himself, he said, "I think I will enjoy having you around. "

Tom gestured over his shoulder, "You know, I would have put my wet clothes in one of the branches of the tree over yonder way. She can't climb trees!" He snorted at his own joke. "You turn the other cheek now," Tom walked away laughing.

Bill washed his clothes again, and then hung all of them in the branches to dry, as Tom had advised him. Though, he was not a hundred percent sure that dog, wouldn't find some way to climb the tree.

While waiting on his clothes, he decided to take a walk. Who would see a half-naked skinny man out here, anyway?

He walked down the slope, toward the morning sun. He stopped on a large granite outcropping and stretched out on it. This piece of stone hung out over the hillside by twenty feet. It looked as if it were one hundred feet down if one were to fall or jump.

"What beauty!" Bill said to the landscape and no one else.

As he was gazed out, he admired red hawks flying up and down and all-around riding the thermals of the airstream, likely looking for a plump looking rabbit, or maybe a rat.

His mind went into autopilot. He forgot about his childhood, his rise to power and his hard fall from grace. He forgot that he had no family, nor a job.

He rested his mind on the arm of the mountain, and it soothed him.

He dreamed someone was calling his name from far off.

10 – HAPPINESS FOUND

"Bill, where are you? Did you jump off the hill without your clothes? What an idiot! Suicide is bad enough, but you going to do it half-naked?"
"I've been fixing breakfast for two! That's me and you. Where in Blue Blazes are you?" Tom was hollering at the top of his lungs.

Slowly, Bill came around. "Tom, I'm over here. Give me a few minutes, and I'll eat your breakfast."

His mind was blank, and he had obviously lost track of time.

He chuckled to himself.

He stopped on his way to pick up his clothes to decide what was bothering him. He couldn't figure it out. Moving up the slope, he caught himself whistling.

"Wait!" His heartfelt light. "I'll be damned, I'm happy." For the first time in years, he felt good.

He grabbed his mostly dried clothes and ran up the slope to the shack, to find Tom indeed had breakfast. There was enough food on the table to feed a platoon of hungry people. Eggs, thick slabs of bacon, flapjacks, toast, honey, etc. Hot Black, coffee, too. He did not notice any sugar, but he noticed Tom poured in a healthy amount of honey into his coffee. Bill decided to follow Tom's lead.

Bill had noticed a couple of ice chests in the shack but had not seen any other foodstuffs on his way out of the house. He thought Tom must be a magician with food storage to have all of this safely stored away and to keep it from spoiling. His 'stove' was an old Coleman camping style mounted waist-high on stacks of books.

Bill thought, "oh well if that stack catches fire, this place will not last 30 minutes. I guess there will not be much lost except the books."

Bill's stomach screamed. How long had it been since he had eaten? He jumped onto the stack of books that Tom had put in place for him to sit upon, as there was only one wooden chair in the 'kitchen'.

He grabbed food from the table and shoveled it onto his plate. He quickly bowed his head, and said a short prayer, and proceeded to eat.

Tom said, "If you were giving thanks, I am the one that cooked it."

Bill replied, "Yes! Thank you for cooking breakfast! Of course, God created all of this."

"Yeah, well I put in the butter and fatback. That's why it tastes good!" Tom retorted. "The honey came from outback. I got a few beehives back there."

"It's wonderful," Bill said with his mouth completely full. Small pieces of food fell from his mouth while he tried to talk, chew, and swallow all in one move.

"How long has it been since you ate? You need to slow down a little before you go missing a finger or two." Tom asked Bill, obviously concerned.

"I am not sure, seems like forever. A few days?" Bill replied, between fork-fulls.

"Well, you ain't going to starve around me! I'll make sure you eat ok. Man has got to eat right, otherwise his animal instincts take over." Tom said.

Tom got a thought, and of course, talked it out.

"Why, you take food away from a gentleman. Give him about three weeks with nothing but water. Put him in a situation where someone else and he are starving together. Then give them just enough food to last one of them a couple of days."

Tom pointed one hand at Bill, " Do you think that food will last? Likely as not, one of them 'ill kill the other. What do you think about that? Doya' think you can pray to your God with your belly crawling and wiggling against your backbone?"

11 - THE SCIENCE OF GOD

Reverend Bill did not know what to say.

His mouth fell open, his mouth sputtered spilling food, before finding words.

Bill asked, "Do you not believe in God, Tom?"

"Of course! I am God! I already told you that," Tom smiled behind his beard. "Just not in the way that you do. Hmm, now you believe I am nuts.
Right?"

Reverend Bill took a breath and began, "Trust me. I have much experience in helping people find God. And, I can tell you right now, the before and after person is awe-inspiring. When a Nonbeliever becomes a Believer, it is a wonderful thing to behold."

Tom shakes his head to the affirmative, his beard moving up and down his belly.

"So's, try this on for size. And, just for repeats, bear in mind, I ain't had an education you might know of. But I read and I mean, a lot!" Tom leaned forward placing his hands on his knees.

"Scientists tell you that the universe was created from the

'Big Bang.' They say that all this goop was spinning around in the universe, some 14 billion years ago, with nothing else around it. At some point, this stuff pulled in on itself by gravity and centrifugal force, into a tiny point they call a 'singularity.' The singularity was incalculably dense." Tom's hands came together in a squeezing action.

He continued, "At some point, it generated enough heat to cause a huge explosion. All this stuff went spinning off from the middle of the explosion into the universe. 'Big Bang'!" Tom's hands moved quickly away from each other to demonstrate the bang. "After a pot full of years, some of this exploded crap started to cool, and come together, or coalesce. Some of this hard goop started spinning around and sucking in other stuff getting denser with huge gravity fields. Eventually, enough heat got generated from all of this for a fusion reaction to start."

His hands came together in a cupping action, "Presto, the stars. Our sun is supposed to be around 5 billion years old. So, it is a newer one. A baby. But that means some of the other stars in our galaxy and others could be 10 to 14 billion years old. Some smaller pieces of goop started to circle these stars and finally cooled. Planets? Right? Supposedly earth is over 4 billion years old!"

"Another pot full of years goes by and more chemical reactions take place, combining and stewing!"

Tom slapped his hands together,
"Pow!" Tom exclaimed and Tilley jumped, looking at him as if she needed to do something. "Life! True, it was probably a single cell at first and a long way from Wall Street. But the longest journey starts with that first step."

Tom, as was his custom, didn't wait for any kind of response, but Bill was amazed, nonetheless.

Tom waited for a microsecond or so, and said, "Sounds to me like everything came from the same goop. A little different packaging, but the same stuff."

Bill had truly thought Tom was ignorant based on his speech and lifestyle. It was now obvious he was wrong. This is a common mistake that most of humanity make at one time or another when presented with someone different from themselves.

Tom's eyes gazed at a point above Bill's head, and continued, "What if this stuff were God? Let's say he sat there for a few trillion years. He got bored, you know, with nothing to do, no one to talk to, no gambling, no football games, and so forth." Tom extended both arms and went on, "Maybe he went a little crazy and just exploded, or maybe a little dust got up his nose and he sneezed! The scientists would still have the "Big Bang" theory, and I would still be God."

12- THE BIG BANG
AND LIFE

Bill's mind was in a whirl trying to keep up, trying to see where this diatribe was going.

Tom continued to explain, "I mean if you get a drop of water from the ocean, wouldn't it still be water? So, I am a small piece of God, therefore, I'm God. You're God, and Sara's God, and the 'Good Book' is God, and so on!"

Tom was really ramping up now, "Think on this. Why would God only create one planet with life?"

" Let's say that our Milky Way Galaxy has 200 + billion stars. What are the statistical chances that out of the 200 billion stars, that none of them have a planet like the Earth? Big Brains call this the Goldilocks theory, for life! The planet must not be too hot or too cold! It also has to have liquid water!"

Tom continued, "Some stars have no planets, others have more. NASA and other scientists are proving this. Let's say that each star has an average of four planet-like objects. From what the astronomers tell us, there's more, but I like round numbers. That means there are 1 Trillion planets possible in our galaxy alone. Let alone the other thousands of galaxies we now know to exist."

"Now, how many of those are Goldilocks planets with the

chance of life? Let's just there is only 1 percent. So, now our chances are only 1 billion? Out of that number, how many have life advanced enough to call it civilized? One percent or 10 million? Man, those are a lot of chances for civilization in this galaxy alone."

"Now, there is a formula, developed by a man named Drake that takes much more into consideration. My way is crude. But it shows the same kind of thing, which is life is not only possible, it is likely. By the way, the Drake equation estimates an even higher possibility of life and civilizations than I just did."

Bill found his thinking was now catching up. He began to understand, via the numbers what Tom was proposing. Even though on the surface, it appeared to contradict his beloved Bible, he began instead to understand that God's presence was much bigger than one small planet in the corner of the small Milky Way Galaxy.

Tom looked very seriously at his hands, and said, "If you think that there might be one chance in a million, that still leaves hundreds upon hundreds of planets like Earth. That's an awful lot of chances for life. What do you think?"

Reverend Bill's mouth sputtered to life and tried to say something intelligent. "Nowhere in the Bible does it speak of another Earth."

13 – CIVILIZATION

Tom took off again, "Ok, I give you that."

"But it opens up another point. What about religion? Well, the way I see it, some people use their common sense and others don't. Like a street sign warning you to stop for cross traffic. Some people will have the horse sense to slow down and look for oncoming traffic. Most won't. They'll be wrapped in making money, poking the old lady, finding nirvana, whatever. So, now we have a potentially bad situation where people get hurt and die. Worse yet, they act like animals and are not 'civilized.' The biggest bullies among us corrupt people around them to kill masses of people. Hitler and the Nazis, 6 million Jews dead. Stalin, in his genocide state-run programs likely tops 10million people killed. Building a 'pure race' with your desirables while destroying those that are different has been a hobby of horrible humans since the beginning." Tom now looked directly at the floor where a novel lay. Mark Twain's, 'Huckleberry Finn.'

Tom extended his right hand to Bill and asked, "How do I prevent these idiots from killing each other? So, religion is a set of rules to guide all of us into treating other people and themselves, OK. You could say religion is the basis of civilization!"

"For instance, don't covet thy neighbor's wife, don't kill, and so on. These are all good rules for us to live by, but a lot of people don't have the sense to follow them. Now we include heaven as a positive reward and hellfire to get their attention! Just for a comparison, look at what happens in the Communist countries, where the bigshots get to eat and kill the small people, while the small people just want to live and find something to eat! Religion is not much allowed in those countries since Communism is so 'intelligent.' As a matter of fact, it is fairly normal for the elite and intelligent ones to deny God. "

Tom's emphasis showed heavy sarcasm towards the word, intelligent.

"Hell, there was a famous writer that said something like, even if there is no God, mankind would have to invent one! Asimov, I think!" Tom finished.

Reverend Bill wanted to eat, but Tom had him under his spell.

Tom stopped gesturing and began to stroke his beard, "You know, I had a mule that you had to hit every day on the skull, with something hard to get his attention. All day he would pull the load, but the next morning you had to scare him a little. I ain't sure if he enjoyed the hitting or if he forgot overnight that I was going to do it."

Tom's eyes and head turned to the floor while his hands crept up to his ears cupping his face.

"Lost him last year. Felt like I lost family!" Tom paused for a moment.

Suddenly his hands went up and now Tom's face had surprise written upon it. "Humph! Can't believe I said that! Damned ole mule. I don't think I ever cussed more than around that old mule." He stared at Mark Twain on the floor again, "I called him Caesar! Stubborn old shit."

With a wave of his hand, the mule was put behind. "So, mankind is like that Mule. Got to scare 'em now and again to keep them working properly!"

"Anyway, even if God didn't exist, isn't it nice to believe that he, she, it does? Sort of comforting, ain't it, to think that someone or something is actually in control of this mess." Tom finished up.

Bill was ready for this. "The Bible was guided by the hand of God. Everything in it is the truth. Trust me, I know the Bible and I know God."

"Of course, you do. No doubt about it." He reached down, picked up the old cast iron skillet, and thrust it near Bill, "Ya want some more eggs?"

Tom was obviously through with his religious lecture and was not going to argue.

14 - RATTLE SNAKES

Tom stood up quickly, followed by Bill.

Bill grabbed the dirty plates and utensils and began to clean them in a small bucket with a little soap and water. He was determined to show his gratitude by helping Tom out.

Tom said, "Thank you for that. I'll be going down the hill to Brenda town in a bit. Nice little town, with just a few permanent folks. We passed the cutoff for it on the way here. Ain't a whole lot to see other than Motorhomes and RVs, but the ghost town is still standing. It goes way back to the 1870s, I think. There is also what is left of the gold mining operation, and 'God's Little Church in the Desert.' That church is famous. Ya know? Some little things to see. If you want to go, you'd better get a move on. You want some more coffee?"

Reverend Bill was not sure that after such a good breakfast he was ready for another kidney busting, slow turning ride in Sara, the Truck. And, getting cooped up in the truck with Tom's aroma did not appeal to him.
Finally, he probably had eaten way too much, after such a long time without eating.

"Tom, I believe I'll stay here, let my food settle and look around. That is if you think you can trust me not to burn the place down. I am tired of moving, and I feel good here. I feel God here! And, despite your logic, I need to pray a little."

Tom said, "OK! You got it. I'll miss your company, though! You're a Hell of a talker!"

Tom had already turned his back moving towards the truck, Sara.

"Don't forget to pay attention to Tilley. She needs more than I have given her lately since I ain't been around much. UH, keep your fingers away from her mouth for a few days. Just in case, you know?" Tom said, with a little wink.

Tom bent over, picking up his equipment, and moved to the truck to put it into the bed. He pulled the brick from the tire and jumped quickly into Sara to brake her.

"Oh, by the way, stay away from the rock by that big Joshua tree, just North of the house. It ain't safe! I ain't going to come back here and haul your butt down the slope to a Doc. And watch for snakes! They love this time of year, and they 'specially love tender-foots, that don't know where they're laying."

He turned back to Bill,

"By the by, there's one rattler that loves that rock you were on this morning!"

"You there in your underwear and all! Hell, you might have given him a start. Or maybe, just a giggle!"

He turned Sara over, she caught, sputtered, and died. He turned it over again until she was ready to roll. With a repeat of the sounds from yesterday, the truck began to move down the hill.

Bill watched as the old truck moved, bouncing, sputtering, and belching a cloud he could see long after the truck had gotten out of sight.

15 - HAPPY REVEREND BILL

Bill said out loud to Tilley, "I guess I need to look around a bit! Been a long time since I was in a house. But then I am going for a walk to work off some of this breakfast."

Tilley seemed to understand as she went to the door and lay down outside.

Bill walked once completely around the shack, then went inside. He made a quick accounting of the shack.

There were only two rooms. One, about eight by eight feet, was Tom's bedroom, with hundreds of paperback and hardback books piled on every horizontal surface. The bed was carved out, so Tom had a place for his body. The books in this room included biographies, history, romance novels, science fiction, even self-help books. The Genre covered every conceivable author and situation one could think of. There was also a well-worn Bible. The large kind that most people put in their living rooms.

Bill opened the cover, looking for the page that dated and named all your kin.

Tom's Bible had that page torn out, which Bill found to be curious.

The other room was a combination kitchen, living room, and now, bedroom for him. It was a little larger at eight feet by eleven.

Neither room's ceiling was much taller than Tom. He felt the need to stoop slightly as he walked around.

Many of the things Bill noticed in these rooms, were books as well. He noticed that the books that had been his chairs were physics and chemistry books, while the breakfast table was, mostly war and spy novels.

This man loved to read indeed! However, there wasn't any evidence of electricity, therefore, there were no radios, televisions, or any other modern appliance. Tom obviously did his cooking and reading by candle or kerosene flames. Bill found little evidence of clothes, either.

Where did his money come from? There were no unused or used envelopes. Bill assumed that Tom did not get government assistance as a likely 'drop-out'. From the tools in the back of the truck, Sara, Bill assumed he did odd jobs for people.

Bill based this on the fact that Tom obviously dropped everything on the floor. This would surely include a government envelope or check stub.
He must work solely in cash, or perhaps trade.

He further assumed that Tom was nothing more than a cultural drop-out. Maybe, even a crook.

But, no! That can't be. The guy is too full of love and life.

Reverend Bill walked back out and wandered up the slope with Tilley trailing nearby, just out of his reach, but close enough to hear her. He got the distinct impression she was watching his every move, just waiting for him to do something wrong so Atilla could come out.

He prayed as he walked, giving thanks to God for all his life and Polecats' introduction to it.

At the same time, part of his conscious brain admired the beauty of what was around him. He rounded another large outcropping of rock and slowed down. There was a huge tree there beside a small watering hole fed from the same spring he had washed his clothes. Murmuring water sent soothing sounds to Bill's ears.

He decided to sit on the rock and let the world pass by.

Birds flew overhead, small red hawks dove for field mice and lizards, and he saw other desert creatures going about their business. He began to feel the lives that were around him.

The air smelled wonderful and fresh. He floated with the world, and as it turned in space, so did he.

He thought about what Tom had said about everything being a part of God.

No wonder Tom was so happy being alive. He didn't seem to regret one thing about his life. And, he had all this natural beauty in eye's view.

16 - THE OLD ONES

Tilley had lain down near him for a time but later left.

Bill never noticed. Shadows grew longer on the ground. Twilight came.
Still, Reverend Bill sat, mesmerized.

Bill felt something around his chest. He groggily glanced down, remembering Tom's warning of snakes.

Around his arms, over his chest, was a rope. He didn't like this as it was breaking up his 'feel good'! Bill felt increasing pressure as if the rope was pulling at him.

Bill saw the ground coming up to greet him. He had been pulled from his rocky seat onto his chest.

As he hit the ground, the air rushed from his lungs, and he heard a grunt issue from his body. He felt a whirlwind in his brain like his nerves were having tremendous traffic jams in his mind. The earth was moving past him.

Now, he was being dragged, on his chest.

Tom had the rope and was pulling Bill towards him, with Tilley running around and barking like her namesake.

Tom pulled him roughly to his feet. Bill could see his lips move but could not hear his words. He couldn't hear anything, as a matter of fact. Slowly, the whirlwind in his mind went away,

51

and sound began to return to his ears, but he seemed to be falling.

"You idiot! Didn't I tell you to stay away from here? This is exactly where I told you not to go. What in blue blazes do you think you are doing? You don't know what power you might have un-leashed!" Tom continued to rant and rave.

Bill faded away, losing consciousness.

Bill was thrown over Tom's back, like a sack of flour and was carried like this until they arrived back at the shack.

Tom gently placed Reverend Bill back on to his cot, like a child into its crib. Bill barely felt any of this.

Tom watched over him for three days, before Bill awoke. Tilley was sniffing at his hand. His head had a band of pain just above his eyebrows, and the sunlight was harsh to his eyes. Bird chirps hurt his ears.

Bill asked, "What's going on? How long have I been asleep?"

Tom gently said, "You shouldn't have been there! I tried to warn you away! The Old Ones used to use that Gate after years of meditation, prayer, sacrifices, and preparation. You might have died there. Worse, you may have let loose energies on the world that might have changed everything you call reality!"

"What? Are you nutts?" Bill asked bluntly.

"Well Yeah! We have already covered that!" Tom stated. "The toothpaste is out of the tube!" Tom responded, "But, my mental state has nothing to do with God's Gate!"

Bill's eyes were wide open, and his jaw was hanging slack, now.

"Wait! Slow down. Can I get a cup of coffee? Have you got any aspirin?" Bill was almost begging. "Tell me again, what you said, slower and more quietly!"

Tom found him an aspirin bottle and gave him several. The

coffee had been brewing, and Tom poured Bill a large cup.

Bill downed three aspirins firstly, followed by a healthy but guarded gulp of coffee, without honey. He was not sure that his head could wait long enough for the honey to pour.

Tom began slowly, more seriously than Bill had seen him talk before.

"When I first got here, decades ago, it was through that gate. The one you fell asleep on. Its strength comes and goes. Right now, it seems to be getting stronger. I hope that is a good sign. You see, it is a force of nature and God. You hop on the gate in one place and land in another!" Tom said. His eyes searched Bill's face for understanding.

Tom started again, "Physics geniuses would call it akin to a Black Hole. A wormhole. Picture a spiraling tunnel through space. But it comes and goes without sucking everything in like a Black Hole would! Some might call it a portal. To me, it is a gate!"

"You see! The Old Ones used these for millennium to travel vast distances." Tom said.

He decided to ignore the impossibility of some things that Tom has said, and ask a simpler question, "You say, 'Old Ones'. You mean like Old Indians?"

Tom said, "No, the Old Ones weren't from around here. They were from out there. "Tom's beard and chin pointed toward the cosmos. "Older civilizations that had time to grow and develop technologies we have never seen. Remember, our star is much younger than the other stars."

Bill just shook his head. There was too much to swallow right now.

Tom went on, "These gates allowed them to go from place to place and lose very little time. So, rather than traveling in a straight line in a spaceship, like we would, which would take forever, you bend space and time, like folding a sheet of paper. From the tiny bit I remember, these gates exist in most places of the universe in varying degrees of intensity and duration."

"There are plenty of other so-called gates in various places in this world. Peru, Greece, and so on. Myths surround all of these, with tales of very intelligent beings that come out, usually called "The Gods". And, since the ancient cultures did not understand the technology, they revered "The Gods". You know? Since technology sufficiently advanced is just like magic to the lesser ones. They must be Gods!" Tom waved one hand in a circle for emphasis.

"For instance, there is a Pacific Island called Tanna, whose residents worship our Soldiers and Air Force of WWII. There was a temporary airbase there then to fight the Japanese. The soldiers likely gave the residents coffee, chocolate, cigarettes like you have heard of in other theatres of war operations.
The Natives were quite primitive, so their first bout with the outside world was men in flying ships, with fancy clothes and weapons."

"They have festivals where they wear crude replicas of the US uniform, flag, and they have a crude representation of an American war plane to this day. The festival is called John Frum. Likely, John Frum was a soldier they really liked that promised to come back in an airship and reward them."

"So, these "Gods" seemed to come and help the local population to advance and then disappear. Whole populations have disappeared quite a few times in history. An entire village in Northern Canada even dug up their dead and apparently took them with them never to be seen again. As to the Mayans, we can only guess at what happened to them at their end. Their cities were abandoned without direct cause and the mass disappeared. College boys will tell you in most of these cases they had overused their environment and a simple drought drove them out. "

One hand pointed down at the floor now, "Or, here in the Southwest, you have ancient cliff dwellings of the Anasazi. We have no idea why they built homes into the cliffside, nor why they left them. Big Brains like to say the cliffside dwellings allowed more land for farming. If you see the place for yourself, you will question that one, as it would appear they were hiding from something that was above them. Easter Island is another famous one, that had a large native population in the 1700s chronicled by Captain Cook. But they seemingly disappeared later. Our professor folk will say, they too overused their environment. We do know they came to know cannibalism from various bones left around."

"China has unexplained missing populations with huge underground places carved out for some purpose and no sign of people. Indeed, it has happened all over the world."

Bill had to interrupt, "Hold on. With me, there must be motivation. What possible motivation could these beings, the Old Ones, to come and help us? Are we just future food for them?"

Tom chuckled at the thought, "You know, there was a Science fiction TV show way back in the '60s that had that as the storyline. It was about an alien cookbook on how to prepare and serve man."

Tom got serious again, "But, no. I don't think so. DNA scientists cannot figure out what took place some 65000 years ago, as there was a very dramatic change in our DNA that caused our brains to be larger, among other things. And, they found one DNA strand from 45000 years ago that seems to be uniquely distinct from Neanderthal, Cro-Magnon, and all the rest of humanity."

Tom raised both hands and dropped them back to his lap, "So, IF you believe in life outside our spaceship earth, and IF you believe there could be life more advanced, then you can guess as to motive."

Tom paused, poured himself and Bill another coffee, and

stood rather than regaining his seat.

"My belief and others are they seeded us to grow and advance away from caveman Neanderthals into Homo Sapiens, becoming more intelligent and closer to 'civilized'. I believe the overall goal for the Old Ones is to find life that could be sentient, test it, change its DNA, such that eventually, it will grow into a functioning and advanced race of beings. My bet is most races eventually develop the technology to make a nuclear bomb, just to kill their enemies. By that process no doubt, many blow their world apart. So, even at the time of their invention, they prove their stupidity by killing themselves with it. "

Tom paused to make a point, "You know, this world has had several close calls with nuclear weapons."

"So, to me, that is the overall motivation. i.e. to guide a promising race on a planet to see if they can become useful to the universe as a whole. The losers die, the winners gain everything. Ones too violent and stupid never make it out there to join the rest of the gang." Tom again pointed to the ceiling with his chin.

17 – STONES

Bill was starting to get the hang of this but still felt an incredible doubt in all of it. But Tom was so emphatic.

"Our big brain scientists still cannot figure out how the early Egyptians could build the pyramids with copper tools carving granite, for God's sake. Granite is so hard and dense, only diamond tip tools would work. And, if one examines some of the stone works around the world, the symmetry and accuracy of those cuts defy logical explanation. We would require computer-aided tools to match the accuracy and with our present CAD machines, it would still be very difficult. Copper tools, no!"

"Or ask yourself how the ancients transported stones that easily weighed 20 tons to 100 tons. Oh, historians explain it away with many many slaves, but that really does not work for me. A decade back, a Los Angeles museum had to transport one stone that approached 40 tons. Huge cranes had to be used and then a horrifically modified flat-bed trailer had to be constructed to transport that boulder. Traffic had to be dealt with from Arizona, down I-10 to California. It was a huge engineering feat that took a lot of resources."

Tom shook his head, ran a hand through his beard, and started again,
"These huge tons of stones not only show up in Egypt but in many places around the world. Stonehenge in the U.K. Machu Picchu

in Peru. The Temple of Apollo at Delphi in Greece." Tom's arms showed a sweeping motion.

He continued, "In many of these places, the local Myths tell us the stones were floated into place. I guess I have to call bullshit on that one. There is even one place in Florida that has huge coral rocks carved into shapes. One small 100-pound man supposedly built the 'Coral Castle' by himself. There too, are stones of 20 tons and more. How did one guy move those? The builder, Leedskalnin, would only say he had discovered the secrets of the Egyptians. He worked only during the night, by himself, so no one has a clue how he did it. It still exists today if you would like to see it for yourself and marvel at the impossibility."

Tom began to pace a bit, back and forth, while his eyes ran around the room. "Other curious things are like the pyramids which show up in various places around the world, not only Egypt, but also in parts of Mexico, China, and recently in parts of Europe. NASA satellite data indicate one might exist in Antarctica. What the hell?"

Tom moved a hand over his face, while Bill seemed stunned.

"Now, if all humankind spread from one place in Africa over hundreds of thousands of years, and separated, how did these cultures happen onto such related building construction?"

Bill suddenly spoke, "They all came from the Garden of Eden, it says so in the Bible. They began as one people. Simultaneous inventions have happened many times in our history. Our own U.S. patent office can prove it. I think it was 126 times from the beginning of the patent system that separated people invented the same thing. The telephone, for instance, Bell and Meucci."

Tom said, "Ok, I will give you both Eden and patents, as well. So's you are saying building techniques could have happened at the same time. Good!"

Tom continued, "Now, when Cain slew Able and was cast out of Eden, he went to the land of Nod east of Eden, where he married a woman, and she gave him Enoch in birth, Noah's great great grandfather. Where do these new people come from in the land of Nod? This land of Nod, nor the people are mentioned in the Bible until after the slaying."

"Please understand, this is of no disrespect to the Bible or any of the stories in it. They can be 100% factual about everything and yet there are holes. I personally believe God and Jesus to be real. But it does not explain the entire history of mankind or the 4 billion years preceding the Bible. Mankind is not the Biblical 3800 years old. One of our ancestors, Lucy, is said to be 6 million years old. Lucy was a skeleton found by a man named Leakey around 1974."

"Or, take the case of huge quantities of liquid mercury found under ancient buildings in widely spread locations. What in the hell would ancient man do with liquid mercury? Today, we use it for its electrical properties. There is a belief that the one in China used Mercury to mimic water flowing. The one in Mexico for a God ceremony. Both had thousands of gallons of deadly mercury."

"Anyway, the last ice age ended some 12,000 years ago, which is really funny. Why? In Turkey, an ancient site was found by accident in the mid-'90s at an altitude of 2500 feet above sea level. It was dated to 12,000 years old. It is called Gobekli Tepe and has many huge stone carvings that are 10-20 tons with beautiful reliefs of various animals carved into them. Some of the animals on the stones never existed in Turkey but did in other parts of the world. Lots of questions there, with very few answers."

Tom paused, but then waved both arms in exasperation.

"Again, it was' Some kind of Temple', the college boys tell us. I have no idea how many slaves would have to be used to build that place, but it would take many more to bury it, and it was buried on purpose. To this point in time, no one knows who built it, what tools they used, who they were, or why they tried to cover it up."

Bill interrupted his flow. "You know, I had a seventh-grade science teacher that just blurted out one day that civilizations had existed before this one. I never understood what he was getting at until now." Bill was shaking his head as if to clear something in his mind.

18 - GATES

Tom stopped, took a breath and started, "Anyway, regardless of all of that early construction, and Biblical accuracy, the normal mind cannot cope with the gates. My bet is if a hundred people decided to try it out without training, there would be a hundred dead people."

"The state of your mind is mostly how you ride the thing safely. That is why the Old Ones prepared themselves for so long. If you went into the mainstream with anger on your mind or revenge, your exit might have an explosive force capable of a bomb. If you were on one of the side streams, you might just fry everything within a few hundred yards. If you went in with fear, you could lose your mind before your exit. Your mind has to be quiet, placid!" his hands went still.

"You see, the gate is like a river of energy, with some currents being faster, or stronger than others. You were sitting on the very edge. That is probably what saved you." Tom finished.

Bill mulled this over in his mind as much as he could behind the pain in his head.

Tom said, "The Hopi Indians from these parts have stories and myths about strange people coming in and going through the gates that sometimes-shared tremendous wisdom with them!"

Bill offered, "As in the angels? In most ancient texts and the

Bible, these were called the Watchers. At different points in the Bible, an angel would appear to help someone and pass a message from God."

"Good, thank you for that," Tom said.

He went on, "The stories said they looked somewhat like us, but were either taller or much shorter. In some of the stories, around the world, their heads were larger and longer. Strangely enough, in Peru scientists have found elongated skulls missing the sagittal suture, common to Homo Sapiens. That is not a clue to pass over. Now, you could make the statement it was a fault of local DNA, but there is not just one skull like that, but a few dozen, missing a human connection of the sagittal suture."

"And, in Egypt, there was a real funny looking King and his sister who are always carved or painted with funny looking heads and bodies. Akhenaten was his name. Bad DNA, inbred caused? Don't know." Tom shrugged his shoulders.

"The Indians around here painted what they saw on big rocks throughout this part of the country! I have seen a few of these drawings on rock walls." Tom used his hands to demonstrate some of the shapes. "College boys call them Petroglyphs. Hopi Indians have stories about 'Ant' people that may be related! Sometimes, they talk about 'Star People'! "

Tom paused just for a breath, then continued,
"The Hopi legends say we are in our fourth world right now, three destroyed before! The first world was destroyed by fire, likely a supervolcano like 'Old Faithful'. The second by ice, which could have been a pole shift. In Antarctica, below the three miles of ice, remains of plant and animal life have been found, so Antarctica must have existed in a different place a long time ago where the air was warmer, instead of where it is now with ice over most of the continent. You know all of the continents are on plates that can move and have?" Really Tom was not waiting for an answer.

He went on, "The third world was destroyed by flood,

maybe the melting of the ice. And, the Hopis claimed these Ant or Star people helped them survive by taking them underground, bringing them out when the danger had passed."

Tom looked directly at Bill now and said, "I hope you realize that though your Bible has the story of Noah, virtually every ancient culture in every corner of the world has a flood story."

Tom's chin pointed up toward the ceiling, again.

"Again, no matter what you call them, they were from out there!"

Cold Ice slipped down Bill's spine. Goosebumps grew on his arms, and his breathing became very shallow.

He suddenly understood something that had been missing.

"Hold it right there! How did you say you got here?" Bill asked.

19 – POLECAT'S PAST

Tom drew a ragged breath, and said, "Through God's Gate, I said! I was nothing but a teenager. I was way too young and stupid to climb onto the thing, nor did I have a tenth of the knowledge needed to survive. Apparently, I had been watching other travelers, or maybe I was getting taught, I really do not remember. But I knew enough to climb on without clothes. I believe that is necessary if you don't have specially made suits."

Tom's eyes changed like they were looking far away.

"Anyway, when I came out, I had forgotten who I was, and where I had come from. The power of the gate took my memory from me like a big magnet could be used to erase magnetic data on a tape."

Bill found himself startled at the word 'tape'. He had a memory of something called magnetic tape that was obviously used in the past for music, movies, and computers.

Tom turned his whole body to face a Northern direction, which led back to I-10 like he was physically remembering the way. "After a while, I wandered down the mountain, found the highway, and picked up some clothes along the way passing cars lost one way or the other."

"I learned to hitch rides like you do. I found myself in Bagdad Arizona for a while. I had no idea where I was. I kept my trap shut and listened to other folks! It took me a while to get a hang of the language. What I did remember of my own language would never work here. So, I listened to everyone. I picked out the word, Arizona. I was in Arizona. And, I learned about food names and water. One step at a time, I found out what I needed to know. I did not try to talk to someone for a few weeks. And, when no one was around, and I could speak out loud, I tried to mimic their accents so I could fit in. To practice, you know."

Tom went on, "After a few years, of doing odd jobs and learning the language, I got a hankering to see the world outside Arizona. So, I lied about this and that and joined up with the Marines. I told 'em I was twenty and my folks had died in a house fire, and all of the records were burnt with them. By then, I could read and understand enough English to fake my way. Most just thought I was a backwoods hick. Back in that time frame, electronic records did not exist, and not a lot of young men were joining the armed services. So, I slipped in. You know, there was a lot of physical training in basic training in San Diego. A fellow learned to march and shoot the M-1 rifle, hand to hand combat and so forth. But the mental and emotional load they put on a soldier was a lot tougher on me. Wow! How those drill Instructors screwed with your head. The Drill Instructors, or DIs, would get so close to you that when they screamed at how stupid you were and how ugly your momma was, their spittle would land on your face. No way you could wipe it off. Just had to wear it." Tom made motions with his hands as to where the spittle landed on his face.

He continued, "Basic was very hard on me. I believe I have an inbred revulsion to violence, but I learned what I needed to defend myself and my fellow Jarheads. I never did well as a soldier, just enough to stay out of trouble. The chow was pretty good, and I liked wearing that uniform. Yes siree, I liked that uniform. Anyway, I made it through Marine basic training and later volunteered for sea duty on Navy boats. I know the Navy and Marines were natural rivals, going back through the years, but I never minded the Swabbies myself. This was after WW2 and before the

Korean war."

Tom looked up at the ceiling, slapped his legs with his hands and said, "Man, that was something else, to see that big old ocean and all of those seaports. I found I loved boats and the ocean. Hell, there were a few times we could spot whales and dolphins. That made it fun. I know some people got seasick. Never me. Even if that big ole ocean was pushing my boat up, down, and around. "Tom swirled one hand to demonstrate.

He paused, noting the question in Bill's eyes. "Yeah, I know. I am about as far away from the ocean as a person could get right now. I really don't feel I had a choice in that regard because my road led me away from the water."

Tom continued, "So's, anyway, somewhere around Guam, I began to remember bits and pieces of my life before my travel through God's Gate and arrival here. The bits were almost like a fuzzy dream. Not real! You know?"

"I was in the 1st Division Marines, rifle company. Turns out the Chinese decided to invade Korea in 1950. Prez Truman and General MacArthur had already ordered the rest of my division to ship out from San Diego, so my ship was ordered to join as quick as we could. The earliest my ship landed was a little later than the others by a couple of weeks."

Tom held up one hand with one finger stabbing the air, "First thing was taking Seoul back from the Chinese. A lot of hand to hand there. I saw soldiers sliced, stabbed, shot and blown up. Body parts all over the ground. It was hard to figure out which part went with which, Marine. Anyway, Marines pushed the Chinese back. Seoul was free, again. Adrenalin kept you going, fear kept you fighting. We pushed into the mountains and got surrounded near the Chosin Reservoir in the early part of '51 for some 17 days. We had to fight like hell to get out. Lots of soldiers never did. I bet their remains are still there. Anyway, winter was really bad there. It was usually zero degrees, but there were times it was 30 and 40 below. Jarheads froze to death in their foxholes, long before a Chinese fellow could shoot them. The cold caused our weapons to seize up, too. Here you have a Chinese soldier running and screaming at you, shooting the entire time, and you can't get one little bullet to come out. Scary as hell. Most times, you had to swing the rifle and hope the rifle would free up after you connected with someone's head. Most of the soldiers carrying the M2 especially had problems with the cold. They began to remove the oil from the M2, just so the oil could not freeze. Damned thing still jammed. And, the M2 just did not have enough stopping power to make those drugged up Chinese laydown. So, there was a lot of trading of weapons. Why, it was common for a live Marine to stop over a dead Marine, trade his M2 and ammunition with the dead one for his M1. I did that myself. I carried the heavier M1, but it was so much better than the M2, I just had to ignore the weight. There was a lot of hand to hand combat in Korea." Tom made some motions with his hand like he was wrestling someone else.

He went on, "You just have to imagine the whine of bullets going past a fellow, the howitzer concussions, machine-gun fire and those wonderful Marine Gullwing Corsairs flying over-head. I loved the Corsairs. Even if they did not hit the enemy, their bombs made nice deep holes a marine could crouch down in. I got used to the roar of their engines and would watch where they dropped bombs. But I saw a lot of Jarheads die. Later, the history books recorded 28000 Marines casualties with 4200 dead in the Korean conflict." Tom's hands were making circles now. He seemed to lose himself for a few moments.

He gathered his thoughts, and returned with, "Had a buddy there named Charlie!"

He stopped. Bill's face seemed to surprise him.

"What, you don't believe me? I have not got to the unbelievable part yet!"

67

Reverend Bill sat, considering, and then asked, "Just how old are you, Tom? Korea was a long time ago. There has been one war in Vietnam and a few in the Middle East way after Korea!"

Now, it was Tom's chance to think and ponder an answer.

"I don't think you are ready for my years yet! But let me assure you, the beautiful face and body in front of you have many more miles on it than you think!"

He tried to wink at Bill, but it was more like fur moving on a bear.

"So's, anyway, one day while we were getting hammered by the North Koreans, Charlie got his leg blown clean off just below his knee, by a Chinese mortar shell! I was within twenty feet when it happened. I got hit by some of the shrapnel, but none was life-threatening. Took a couple in my neck, and a couple more in my back. Charlie's was bad though. He was bleeding out like a stuck pig. He was already going into shock when I got to him. Soldiers get some first aid training, so I knew to start pressure on the big vein in his crotch." Tom demonstrated with his hands.

Then continued, "Something came over me! His bleeding slowed down from my pressure on the vein, but then my hands got real warm. I remember feeling sick to my stomach because I could see his insides, like he was open, you know. I even saw this big open vein. I told it to close. It did! I know this sounds crazy, but I have done such a thing a few times since."

20 - HEALING

Reverend Bill had forgotten to breathe.

This very strange man had just spoken what Bill felt like when he 'healed' someone in his life as Reverend Bill. In Bill's case, he believed he had healed several hundred people, at least. He too felt the heat in his hands. He too sometimes saw inside someone's body or brain. Sometimes he saw Cancers, sometimes a bleeder.

Once he had seen a small-caliber bullet in the brain of a man others thought was 'possessed' by Satan. For all Reverend Bill knew, the bullet was present because of a childhood accident and likely lay dormant most of the man's life only festering in the last few years. And, the festering caused his abnormal behavior, not the devil. He simply 'healed' the tissues surrounding the bullet to isolate it from the rest of the brain. It was obvious the man felt better when he said his headaches were gone.

Tom continued, "Charlie is alive today, I think. He lost his leg but kept his life. He is older than dirt, maybe. Haven't called him in a long time. He can't dance, but he never was what you would call graceful."

" Anyway, bits and pieces of my past started coming back then." Tom finished.

Bill interrupted, "Whoa Tom! This is all very interesting, but you can't expect me to believe all of this. God's Gate? And you stop a bleeding vein with your mind."

Tom was smiling, now, both hands went to a knee and he leaned forward to Bill, "Well, you used to tell people you 'healed' when you were just a kid, now didn't you? Is that any easier to believe than what I did, Reverend Bill?" Tom asked.

Bill began to speak, then shut up, then began again, "I didn't heal anyone. That was the power of God working through me."

Then Bill stared at Tom, "How did you know that? The Reverend and healing part? I haven't told you a thing about that part of my life, Tom. I don't tell anyone about that part of my life!"

Tom smiled, "You speak without words! We all do! Some people know how to listen. I assume I was taught how to do that as a child, in another place and time, apparently!"

Tom said, "You see, many people can't believe in things they can't touch unless they learn about it as children when they still can believe in anything. That is the reason why you want to teach a child, the right way from their beginnings. A child's mind is like a piece of molding clay. You can squish it good or bad. If you teach him or her to be good with people from a young age, he will grow into manhood being good to people. Sown well in seed, beautiful wheat. If you teach a child to respect others, it will. If you teach a child discipline, they will offer the world their talents."

His hands showed the path from child to man.

"But, if you treat a child as if they are the center of the universe and never scold or correct, they will become an asshole, a bully, and will offer much of nothing to anyone else. All they will feel and know will be about themselves. A life wasted and wasteful to all around it."

21 - REMEMBERING THE RETCHED MIND

Bill kept thinking Tom would wind down, as sometimes he seemed to find the end.

Tom was still talking, "I think I was taught to use my mind like a funnel, to receive and channel energy through it. Most of my people could do that much, I think. By doing this as a child, I grew up able to see things, read things, without actually touching them. I believe you must have some natural ability that you developed more while you were preaching."

Tom continued, "Oh, I can't actually read your mind, word for word. But I can see images. Part of your story I knew before I stopped Sara and picked you up. While you were walking down the road, I was receiving images. I knew you were lonely, hungry, and soul-torn." Tom paused here.

"And, I know you think I talk way too much. Can't help that. It is my nature, don't you know? Out here, I talk to the Tilley, Sara, the cactus, the lizards, just about everything."

Bill felt embarrassment spread through his face realizing he had probably insulted Tom with his previous images.

As he continued, Tom's stare became more distant, "I can't get around a lot of people, because their thoughts can be hard on

me. I was so lucky I
could not 'hear' folks while I was in Korea, but it did begin there. The suffering, the dying. If I could hear their minds then, like I can now, I would have likely gone insane as I never had the training to deal with it. You know? The pain and the fear of dying soldiers would be horrible. I have little doubt there is a way to shut it down, stop listening. But I don't know it."

"So's anyway, after I got out of the Marines, I wandered around a bit with no destination in mind. At the time, I was hesitant to leave my Marine family. Sempra Fi and all. I had all of this structure inside the Marine Corps. I knew what I would be doing and who I would be with all day. You know a Marine never retires. A Marine is always a Marine. We all used to say out loud, 'If I charge, follow me. If I retreat, kill me. If I die, revenge me.' I loved the Marines, though honestly, the killing part never took me. "

Tom was stroking his face again, looking well past Bill. "A really good prez once said, 'Some people spend an entire lifetime wondering if they made a difference in the world. But the Marines don't have that problem.' I kind of like that one. I think it was a Ronnie Reagan quote."

"In Los Angeles, I once stumbled into a poor community and 'heard' way more than I should have. The hatred around me was so strong, I couldn't move. They hated all things white, but many of them hated black too.
I have never understood why people hate someone else just because they look different!" Tom said.

He went on, "So's someone called the cops, and the Police threw me into the drunk tank at the Police Station. I probably did not walk right, probably stumbled. But I wasn't drunk! I was overwhelmed by hate!"

22 - TOM MEETS GOOD

Tom shook his head at the memory and slowly continued. "I thought that I was going to die in that place, listening to what was happening in those guys' heads, both in the cells around me and the cops walking by! I was surrounded by some very dirty and twisted minds. Some were filled with despair, much hatred, and just horrible thoughts. Try to imagine 50 angry people all screaming at you, wanting you to die. And, you could not walk away. I was trapped with them."

"The next morning, a nurse came around. See, some of the drunks had been beaten, some had insides eaten by alcohol, and some just had bad hangovers, so she probably came to the jail thinking she had to try to help those that were slowly killing themselves. I guess the desk sergeant directed her to the worst, as she walked past my cell, never stopped."

Tom smiled a bit and continued, "Her mind felt good and comforted me. She wanted to help everyone, without one thing in return."

Tom slapped both his hand on his knees and continued, "They let me out, that afternoon! The first thing I did was ask the desk sergeant where I could find that nurse."

Tom leaned back, and placed both hands on his ears, "That was a mistake! In his mind, I saw images of small naked children. I think I threw up. They kicked me out of the police station! I remember I stopped a few of their fists with my face before they let me lie still."

"Yet, I was free. So, when I could I picked myself up from the concrete. I knew what I had to do."

"I hadn't read her name tag, but I remembered what her mind felt like.
Every mind seems to have a different tone, rhythm, and sound to it. Think of windchimes where all these different notes blend, caused by the wind to tinkle and sound pretty. Each has its own. Her's was like a small wind chime, where all the notes were high and light. That is what her mind felt like to me."

"I went to the nearest hospital, like a bloodhound sniffing a trail through the woods! As soon as I stepped into the place, I felt her mind. I almost ran over people trying to reach her. She was upstairs. I took those stairs two/three at a time. Three floors up, I saw her. The charity and love in her heart were incredible."

Bill watched Tom's eyes as they began to tear, with drops running down his face, soon lost in his beard.

"She was gently helping an old man get up from his bed. She looked up and glanced at me. Then she gave me a harder look. She had recognized me, I thought, but then I remembered she walked past my cell." Tom's look changed to regret.

"I tried to explain to her I needed to talk to her, but she was frightened of me and called for security. I was thrown out of there, too!"

Tom was rubbing his hands together now, staring again as his shoes. "I was getting the distinct impression I did not belong anywhere around people!"

"In the street, I passed a store window. In the reflection, I realized why I had frightened her. I looked like Hell! I went to a flophouse, paid my six dollars, and took a shower. I washed my clothes in the sink. I borrowed a razor from a guy down the hall and used bath soap to shave. I even combed this mop of mine. I guess I looked and smelled more presentable. Then I went back to the hospital and waited for her to get off her shift. I sat in the lobby, hoping she would come that way. I was afraid there would be a rear exit she might use, but I had already planned to be there the next night if need be. Somewhere at about eight p.m., she came out. She looked tired. I slowly approached her and asked for directions to the pharmacy."

"She didn't fear me this time. She told me how to get to the pharmacy and then asked if I was ok."

"Her mind felt wonderful! I believe even at that moment I was sweet on her."

23 - AMORE

Tom was smiling again, "I asked her name."

"Sheila! Sheila Wilson. I know you, don't I?" Sheila asked.

"Oh, you might have seen me around. Listen, I'm hungry. Could I buy you dinner? There is a nice, small cafe, just down the street. I could really use the company. I bet it's a good place to eat," I smiled my nicest smile, and tried to give her a chance to speak."

Reverend Bill had to laugh to himself at the thought of Tom giving someone else the floor to speak, but then felt embarrassed again, realizing Tom probably read this.

"She said I could, that she knew of the Cafe. We walked together down the street, to the place. She said the cafe was owned by Toni, a friend of hers. He still served good, fresh food, at a reasonable price. We went inside and sat down at the old-fashioned lunch counter. It had those little round stools that you could spin and music things on the counter that you flipped a page at a time to see 10 or so songs. Drop a dime in and punch in the number and your song would play for all to enjoy. The cola dispenser fed in CO_2 to give them fizz, and Toni could add a flavor you wanted. She ordered a Coke with Cherry added in. I ordered a Cherry Coke right after her. A couple of tasty burgers came next. And, to top it all off, we ordered Chocolate Sundays. Though I had been starving, when I left, I was not. Though I was pretty low in the money category, I insisted that I pay."

"It turns out that Sheila had a nice, dry sense of humor and a laugh that was wonderful to hear. Her speaking voice was like silk! Toni had heard her and came right out of the kitchen. Obviously, she was a steady customer, and his smile told me he loved having her there."

"I stared at her brunette hair, which had gentle curves in it." Polecat put both hands around his head to demonstrate, "Sort of, pulled to one side to highlight her face. She had an angelic smile that you could just die for. Blue eyes, that had a funny curve on the top eyelid, while the bottom eyelid was flat. Very intriguing! She didn't wear much make-up at all."

Tom rolled his eyes, "Was I in love? Does the big bear poop where he wants to? You bet I was in love! I am not sure I tasted anything I ate in her presence in Toni's cafe."

"Anyway, I decided I needed to know more about her. We talked and talked, and I asked to walk her home. She told me of a loving mother, but a father that traveled too much and must have been a drinker, as her mother would sometimes shoo her to bed rather than be around him. She seemed to have a lot to say about her mother and more wishes than facts about her father. He must have left when she was still a child. She told me how she wanted to become a doctor, but there simply was not enough money for that, but she had been given an opportunity in the Services as an Army Nurse that must have caught her at just the right time. She said it made her world a reality. She was here, now, as a result of that Army experience and she was profoundly grateful for it. Without a doubt, she loved her life as a nurse."

Tom paused for a bit, one finger finding his cheek just above his beard and casually scratching there. Somewhat absent-mindedly he said, "You know, the world was different then. There were more Americans that were proud of where they lived, and less anger thrown at those that thought differently. In some ways, it was a better time, though the technology side was pretty basic back then. You know. No cell phone thingies."

"Oh, we talked of her favorite singer, Bobby Darrin, singing 'Mack the Knife'. Music had class back then. Musicians not only had passion; they had an education. They honed their music through decades of practice. I asked her what she liked to do when she was not working or volunteering. Knock me over with a feather she said, "Hiking and Painting the landscape." Wow. I asked to see some of her work, and she says, "the next time I see you, I will bring some pieces."

"Oh, and she did the next time. I thought they were wonderful. She brought some pencil sketches as well as small water colored ones. They captured landscapes all right, but it was her paintings of people that I loved. She had one where she captured an old man, a street person in charcoal. Why you could almost believe you saw him alive."

Tom took a long breath and went on, "She tried a couple of times to get me to talk about my folks and where I came from. I would just change the subject or tell how mine was so unimportant. I would have had to lie to her, you know."

"So's, anyway I asked politely if I could see her the following weekend. She told me I could! She suggested the zoo."

"I was ecstatic! I felt like a river running down a mountain slope. I have seen young puppies running and jumping in the spring sun. That's the way I felt! Young and free, and full of love. I went back to my flophouse with my feet barely touching the ground. I didn't have a whole lot of money, didn't have a job, but I was happy!"

"I knew I had to find work. I started at Toni's. Toni was a small fellow, with a gut like you wouldn't believe!" smiled, as his hands rounded his own considerable gut. "I guess he enjoyed his own cooking. But he couldn't hire me. The business was too slow, he says. He was nice though. He suggested a few other places. I tried the gas station down the street, to see if they needed an attendant. Back in those days, you had a little fellow in a uniform that would run out to your car, start feeding it gas, check your fluids, and clean the windows, and all with a smile. At the larger gas stations, you might have several uniformed attendants. But, No! That gas station had too little business as well for them to hire me."

"I tried the VFW to see if they needed someone to sweep the floor. You know, hope for that veteran connection to get me a job. Nope!"

Tom's face took on a forlorn look, as he remembered. Still, his eyes sparkled, as he looked back.

"You get the picture! So, I started taking anything, washing a car for fifty cents, sweeping a garage, fixing a fence, cutting hedges, odd jobs around a house or business, you know? Over time, I had a little money."

"So's, I met her that weekend as I had promised. We decided to take the city bus to the Zoo." Tom was smiling, again. "That was a day to remember. Sheila insisted on paying. "Her treat," she said. I think she knew I had little money."

"I am sure the Zoo and animals were great! Though, my eyes were on Sheila most of the time! We walked around talking about the various animals, had a little popcorn and just enjoyed the day."

"Sheila, well let's just say that Sheila, gave me feelings that were so overpowering, that I just couldn't think straight. As the day wore on, I decided to press her a little, and see what she was looking for in a man or husband. "

"She didn't want to discuss it, but her mind sent me images of gentleness, kindness, all of the good things. I felt encouraged, as I knew I could be those things."

Tom thought for just a minute, and said, "I probably was pressing too hard, too fast. But she was very nice about it."

Tom's smile faded, quickly. "I spent the next two weeks, working odd jobs while she was working and attempting to be with her when she was not."

"There were a few trips for dinner at Toni's and one time we took in a movie. "The Bridge over River Kwai" was the big one, but it was not playing the movie house near us. You might know that back in the 50's Cinema houses rarely had more than one projector, so you only could see the one movie. We saw "Peyton Place" instead. Another big one for that year. That was a wonderful evening." Tom said, "It took me years to get to see the bridge movie, and it was quite more my type than the Peyton Place one."

Tom slumped over then, wearing disgust on his face, "One night, against my better judgment, I opened my big mouth and told her what I believed in. Religion, civilization, the future. I could feel her doubt growing. Couldn't shut my trap! Nope, not me! She thought that perhaps my bread was only toasted on one side if you know what I mean. I never told her where I came from, but no doubt, I sounded strange."

"Anyway, I felt her drawing away from me. She continued to be polite, but, from that moment on, she got further and further away. Another couple of weeks went by, and it was obvious that I was getting nowhere."

"There were a lot of excuses, you see. Over- time, sick friends and more. I saw her less and less. At one point, I know I pushed way too hard for her to go out with me. I think I might have scared her a little because she started crying. Right then, I knew I was done, or she was done with me."

"By the time I finally decided to leave town, I felt almost suicidal."

Tom's face now wandered to look at the ceiling and asked,

"I wonder what she is doing right now? I bet she found some nice guy to marry her, she was too pretty. I hope she is happy."

Again, with his hands moving bad thoughts out of the way he said,

"I wandered for months, hitching a ride when I could, like you. Sometimes going North, closer to San Fran, sometimes going to the coast. You know? Just like a leaf on the breeze. Where I could make a little money, I fixed a few flats and washed a lot of dishes for eats."

"Sometime later I ended up back here. I happened on Interstate 10 and knew my way home. I haven't left again. And I won't until the God's Gate moves again."

"I found Tilley about a year later. She must have been dumped on I-10 and I happened on her before the coyotes got her, though, at her size, hawks could have gotten her as well."

Tilley came near him when she heard her name, and he bent so he could pick her up.

"She was so weak she did not try to run from me. I had to hand feed her at first. But she has done fine ever since. Except, no chickens can be allowed to live here."

Tom shook his finger in Tilley's face, but she did not seem to mind. She licked his finger, and the bear fur smiled again.

24 – MOVE

Tom seemed out of steam, like a balloon, once filled with air but was now deflated.

His head and beard were pointed down now, and still. He seemed to stare out into a space of what life might have been!

Bill thought for a moment, and then asked, "What do you mean you won't leave until God's Gate moves?" He believed that this might change Tom's mood.

Tom responded, "Oh that! Well, you see, the gate only stays in one place for a while. It can evaporate and return, increase or decrease its strength. So, it always moves. It just might not be appropriate to jump on it at any given time, it might not be connected to the other side. I never got the training to understand why or when. I only learned about one-tenth of what I needed. But it has something to do with cosmic energies, gravity waves, solar magnetism, dark matter, and other things. No doubt related to black Holes and string theory. You know?"

Bill had no idea what Tom was speaking of.

"Hey, I am sort of tired. Do you mind if we start up tomorrow?" Bill asked. "My headache is easing, but I must be really tired."

Tom said, "Sure. That is great for me. "

Tom was obviously talked out and likely wanted to forget his past.

Tom started for the kitchen and said, "Good. No more talking. Let me fix something for us to eat, and we will both get an early night."

But, then, he changed his mind, "I have an idea. After we eat, let's go outside and look at the night sky. You will not believe how beautiful it is up there in this part of the country. If we are lucky, we can see a meteor or two streak overhead."

Bill chuckled, "Well, I will be glad to. But you must realize I have been sleeping under that immense carpet of beauty for quite a while now, out in the open. There were times I had no bedroll. Sort of hard to get to sleep, so I watched the stars. But, yes, I will do it with you for a bit." Bill said. "But, just the stars and silence?" Bill seemed to plead with Tom.

Tom did the zipper action across his beard where his lips should be.
He kept his word that night under the mass carpet of a million stars with beauty shown at every turn of the eyes.

25 – REVELATIONS

The next morning Bill woke up before Tom. He decided to walk outside and around, allowing himself time for prayer and to think.

Tom had hit him with a lot of new thoughts, at first forming doubt as to his belief in God and his Bible, but later, firming those same beliefs. Once again, he fully believed in God.

And, the Bible's contents were not just important on Earth, as God likely had other peoples in other places. For Bill, this was a huge mind-bending thought.

What if a person could take the Bible to other worlds, and apply it to other world's language, in their context?

This would mean learning the new world, its civilizations, and history. Rewriting of the Bible would be necessary. But Bill knew he could keep all the fundamental principles the same in the new language.

He knew he was not and could never be Jesus. But he could be Jesus-like, as he always aspired to be. After all, that should be a goal for any person he believed.

He also knew at one time he had had a true talent for preaching and interpreting the Bible. This point of vanity was not lost upon him. His fall from power should have removed all that pride, leaving only confidence in himself.

Tilley kept him company and even seemed to warm up to him. At one point he sat on a rock to watch Hawks spiral and Tilley came near enough to him that her muzzle was just touching his leg.

Without thinking of Tom's warning, one hand went down to rub her behind her ears.

Tilley allowed this touch. It seemed to comfort them both at that moment, with the birds soaring overhead, the clouds quietly moving, while a slight breeze ran in and around the leaves of the Joshua Trees.

"Tom must be up by now. I bet he is fixing breakfast. Tilley girl, you ready to go back?"

Tilley seemed to understand as her tail started wagging. She took the lead home.

26 - GRAVITY

As Bill and Tilley returned to the shack, they could hear Tom whistling, though no musician would have recognized any of the notes.

"Good timing on your part. I just need to toast some bread. Grab your coffee and a plate and fill 'em up." Tom said.

He seemed to be even happier that Bill had seen him before.

They both sat down together, Tom on the single wooden chair and Bill on his pile of books. Tilley ate her food behind Tom.

Obviously, all were occupied with their breakfast, as no words were spoken for a while.

Bill mentioned he had begun to process some of what Tom was speaking the night before. He did not have an education in physics, so much of what Tom said was quite difficult for him to grasp.

"But I believe I did get the thread of what you were saying. And, I believe you had more to say."

Tom stroked his beard and started in again.

"Well, yes, there is a lot more. Are you sure you want to hear more physics? It bores most people." Tom said.

Reverend Bill swept his hands past his knees and up. "I need to understand more. There is a lot of important stuff you have said, and I believe I need a trace of all."

Tom said, "Ok then. But, remember, I am not a big brain, so a physics person could dispute everything I say as inaccurate or wrong."

"Let me start with that genius, Einstein. He set us up for many important things. He developed theories around the 1904 to 1915 era. We still use these today. Just one thing his theory of relativity says is massive objects cause a distortion in the fabric of space-time via their gravity. That was proven. One can't move faster than the speed of light and so forth is another part of that."

"He spent most of his life trying to develop one big theory to explain it all, his Unified Theory. He thought there had to be a relationship between electromagnetism and gravity, as they seemed to be similar. He never quite got it. He chased it his entire life."

"Quantum Mechanics came along later in the '40s and tried to explain behavior at the subatomic levels, particles smaller than protons and neutrons. String theory allows for something called the "Quantum Gravity Theory". I bet Einstein would have trouble with that one, but it might be his answer for his Unified Theory involving Gravitational Waves!"

Bill just stared, but asked, "What are the differences in Einstein and the Quantum thing?"

Tom said, "Well, on a really simple level, Einstein was predicting the four field force behavior at the particle level and larger, while Quantum Theory tries to describe field force behavior at the sub-atomic level. I could say Classical Physics is the macro, while Quantum is the micro to give it a crude feel. Scientists argue Classical works well for the three forces of 'Weak Force', 'Strong Force', and the 'Electromagnetic Force'. It will not work as well with gravity. Many believe a unifying theory will be found within Quantum Theory."

"The world's super colliders are working on the aspects of subatomic forces even as we speak. In the last few years, they have proven the existence of a poorly labeled "God Particle" that only math hinted at. The correct name is the Higgs Boson graviton particle, and the colliders have proven it does indeed exist. Proving the existence of the Boson particle and graviton was crucial to understanding gravity better. Some say a Quantum understanding of the other three forces is more important than Classical Physics understanding."

Tom looked at Bill's eyes and knew he had lost him.

"So, to keep this really simple, I think these wormholes or gates are gravity waves that coalesce and resonant, and bend the fabric of space-time, just like Einstein and Rosen predicted circa 1935. This was called the Einstein Rosen Bridge."

Tom looked into Bill's eyes, "Do you understand?"

Bill let out a breath with a whoosh and said, "I am following some of what you say. I know you are trying to keep this simple and I appreciate it. It is beyond me, though. I know the Good Book more than anything else. When you spend your entire life getting all of your life from one book, you do not pay much attention to other subjects."

Tom started to demonstrate with his hand, bringing them together, twisting them around, "So's these gravity waves resonant you see, rotating together in a single unit'. Picture water swirling around a drain, but much much larger. Now, picture another drain, somewhere else, and its water swirling down. Now, connect those two swirling drains with a swirling tunnel. Presto! The Einstein Rosen Bridge. Got it? The only thing is, it takes massive power for such a thing to exist, way beyond human understanding."

Tom took a breath, stroked his beard and went on, "As Einstein predicted, the massive gravity causes a bending of the fabric of space-time locally. The bending can have a frequency and period to them, like the drain water extending outwards longer. So, when the gravity waves connect someplace, it is like bending a sheet of paper together, through the Einstein Rosen Bridge, and traveling from point A to B is almost instantaneous rather than traveling in a straight line across the universe in a spaceship."

His last gesture was his fingers on each hand touching each other flat, then bending each hand down where the palms touched.

"This is the Einstein Rosen Bridge. Savvy?"

Bill thought he got that one.

"I sort of think God's Gate, or any other portal or gate, concentrates those waves where it touches, and it becomes a river of energy one could ride if one knows how. And, its period must last long enough such they the portal can be detected and used, before it evaporates. It could also explain the many accidental disappearances of people through the ages, where someone watches a person walk into a forest, but could find no clue of them later. One of the first science fiction stories was just after the Civil War, where the writer described just that. In a newspaper interview, he claimed he had seen it, where a friend of his walked into a cornfield, in plain view, then disappeared. So's anyway, it is like they walked into a gate, not realizing it was there and poof, they were gone. Maybe the Devil's Triangle off the coast of Japan and the Bermuda Triangle have temporarily occurring Rosen bridges. According to one airplane pilot, he entered a swirling tunnel at 14,000 feet in a horrible lightning storm and made his journey in one-quarter of the time it should have."

"This Einstein Rosen gravity field is incalculable, no doubt. The density caused in one of these places will be huge and it has to bend space-time fabric. God's Gates carries you through the Worm Holes of the Einstein Rosen Bridge as a result. I think if your mind can hold and ride the energy it will be similar to a leaf floating down with the water current. How a person is not destroyed in it, I have no idea, except you must be in there for just a second. According to present physics, your body should elong-ate, and stretch to the point of oblivion, nonexistence, your very molecules torn apart. Or, maybe your body changes to match the resonant energy till you arrive! Just guessing here, I don't know."

Tom wondered out loud, "Choosing your destination, I bet, is the hardest part! Though I did it once, there is no way I remem-ber how now! Hell, back then I could have been aiming for Alpha Centauri or Orion and I only made it to here! Or, maybe you don't control your destination. Maybe, you just have to know where the gate connects to and decide that is the destination you want to go to. So, maybe it is like having several slides in a playground, and you can select a slide, where you will end up at its bottom, but that is the limit of your choice. I have no idea. And, let's say you want to go back home. You should know how long you are stuck on earth before the next bridge appears or be able to travel to some other bridge to get back home. Some of these bridges might appear once a century, others more frequently. Some fore-knowledge would be necessary to plan your trip here and back home."

Tom rested a moment, then pointed, "Spots like the Joshua tree over there by the rock, is where the gravity waves sort of peter out, like eddy pools in a river, so you can climb out of the river. I've read every physics book from this world I can get my hands on, and just can't figure it out!"

Tom took a breath and went on, "But Quantum Entangle-ment and general theories are just poking the edges right now. You know, two distant molecules that physically react together. One spins one way and so does the other as if paired? Einstein called this "Spooky at a Distance" and never seemed to fully em-brace it. As a matter of fact, Einstein might have believed it to be Bull Shit!"

Bill just stared. He had no idea how to add to the conversa-tion without appearing to be stupid.

27 – HOME GRERSIDAN

"Anyway, I'm waiting for one of the Old Ones to come through. It shouldn't be long now if the Hopi Indian prophecies are true. I've been here so long, though, they might not believe me or help me. They would probably think I was from Earth and not Grersidan."

"Is that where you're from, Tom? Grersidan? How far away is that?" Bill asked.

"I think so. I have the barest memory of Grersidan. With God's Gate, distance is of no concern, of course. None of your star charts have helped so far, either. I thought Grersidan was a small planet in the Orion constellation, but the scientists have only now started to map planets out there. Plus, our names for our planet and yours are very different! So, I am lost!"

Tom seemed to be depressed, again, with the enormity of his task.

It appeared to Bill that if he let Tom talk enough, he would talk himself out.

Twilight came, then the night. Tom had gone silent and finally had gone to his bed. But Bill's mind was wide open in thought! Bill could not help himself! The Revelations of this morning and the discussion with Tom had set his mind on fire.

28 – A TEST OF INSPIRATION

His curiosity drove his feet back to God's Gate in the dark, but the starlight allowed him to see where he was going. As he walked closer, he now knew where the power came from and what it was.

He slowed his pace to understand more of what was happening. Stumbling over a rock might cause something bad to happen if he were to plunge into the energy stream. His plan was to walk closer to the stream than he had before, but carefully. There he would test his own mind and ability.

He knew where he was in the dark by spotting the Joshua tree and the rock.

At fifty feet, he felt a stirring behind his eyes. At forty feet, he felt a pull in the eye sockets and began to feel dizzy. At thirty feet, his mind felt as if he were in a tornado. His ears seemed to hear increasing rushing sounds with every step closer. But, at twenty feet, it changed, all became quiet. The pull behind his eyes and the noise in his ears went away.

He did not hear any critters of the night like insects, the Hoot Owls or Coyotes.

"Maybe this zone dampens sounds. Or, maybe the animals

are repelled by the frequencies. They would likely feel it sooner than a human." he thought.

The silence in his mind was more frightening than he had ever encountered. It was unworldly. In his past, he had spent some time in Caves and Book rooms in underground libraries. They were quiet, but nothing like this. It was not just the absence of sound, but more like the world itself and all connections were blocked off to him.

Bill thought to himself, "This 'location' has cosmic energy connected between planets and star systems. Hell, it probably can move from one galaxy to another. If someone can control the energy you travel. Tom mentioned a peace-filled mind, but I have to guess that knowledge of Star Charts is integral to getting to your destination. Or, as Tom said, maybe you don't control your destination so much as end up at it. But you would have to know where this thing connects to out there. Maybe, computers can predict it?"

He had always thought his mind had acted as a funnel for God's energy when he was a child. Perhaps, he could use this in God's Gate and travel someplace else, using that old talent.

After all, Tom and he shared the talent of healing and seeing inside of people. And, Tom had made it here successfully. Surely, Bill had could have some use of it. He truly felt his mind was un-usual and he just knew he could learn to ride the gate. So, tonight was just to get a feel of the place, and maybe reach out just a tiny bit to the Gate with his mind and see what happens.

He sat on a rock, and began his meditation, calming his mind, trying to control any thoughts of excitement or his body. He had known how to do this before, as his prayers would gener-ally quiet his mind and calm him down. It was old muscle mem-ory.

When his mind was at peace, he thought of the Gate and river, and in his mind, he reached out to it.

Immediately, it was like a switch had turned, and he felt he was getting drawn into the Gate like his mind was leaving his body stretching towards the cosmic river. He felt as if it he was about to rocket away from here never to return.

He knew this was dangerous because he knew he could not control it. He cut off the connection to the Gate in his mind in mere seconds, and the silence and his mind returned to him.

Bill said out loud, "Well, that was a little scary. I am glad I did it. There was an ache around his temples that did not exist just moments ago. So, maybe the Temporal Lobe was used to ride the energy streams?

He thought, "One more time."

Bill spent a few more moments this time to prepare. Now, he knew what the energy stream felt like, and thought he might go just a bit further, a few more seconds to get the feel of it.

When he felt his mind was calm, he reached out to it again. Again, the switch turned and again he felt his mind was pulled, but this time, he felt he could discern colors in the stream, almost like the colors were the strength of the stream. He hesitated to go any further but reached out a tiny bit more to the lighter green stream that was closest to him. Towards the center of the stream it was closer to violet. All colors seemed to shimmer, almost as if they were vibrating. Immediately, the power in his mind was increased and the pull was much stronger towards the center of the stream. He resisted allowing it to pull him further in like he was sliding down a snow-covered slope and was using the heels of his feet to come to a stop.

"Enough", he decided and cut the energy off again. "Ok, that is enough for now. Maybe, I just practice a little every day until I learn more. The problem is if I am overconfident, I will likely end up dead or halfway over the universe."

On the way back to the shack, he had to cross the boundaries in reverse, and they acted the same as when he came down.

"Do I tell Tom or not? I guess I had better not. He was pretty freaked my first time. But, maybe, I can ease him into it. Maybe, he can try the baby steps I just did. But, for now, I will keep this quiet." Bill thought as he walked back to the shack.

29 - EPIPHANY

He found his cot, Tom still snoring nearby, and fell into sleep.

Near dawn, he sat straight up with an epiphany, and a damned strong suspicion!

"Tom! Tom! Get Up! I have to ask you something. By any chance was a God's Gate near Bethlehem, about two thousand years ago?" Reverend Bill asked with high excitement.

Tom was yawning, rubbing his eyes, and trying to wake up.

"What? What in Blue Blazes is wrong with you? Can't ya let a soul rest and wake proper-like?" Tom turned over in his bunk, with his back to Bill, for a moment. Then he turned back. "What are you saying?" Tom sat up while rubbing his eyes and stretching out his back.

When he looked into Bill's eyes, he knew the man was beginning to put two and two together.

"Alright damn it! Fix some coffee and let me wake up, and I'll tell you what I know, and some of what I think!"

Bill did what he was told, quickly. He had to hear this!

After relieving himself outside, and then sipping on his freshly brewed coffee, Tom settled down and began to talk. Tilley came in and lay down next to Tom, with her head in his lap.

"Now Bill, I have no proof of this! I've only been here for some decades. But I have read about the Dead Sea Scrolls, I have read the Bible several times, and I have researched history as best I could. I do believe that Jesus was an Old One. I have no doubt, he was born to a woman named Mary. Mother Mary. Likely, artificial insemination was used for the Immaculate Conception. Didn't you ever think it was funny how little there is in the Bible of him growing? In the Bible, it basically goes from birth to rare moments of his childhood up to a mature man. So, what happens from the age of 12 to 32? No answer."

"I hope in your life you knew that many 'books' were left out of the Bible because they were simply too fantastic for common people to believe in. Sometimes called the Apocrypha Books, these were removed from the Bible. Some of those books had Women in dominant roles. One such describes Mary Magdalene as a prominent disciple. From one fragment with a couple of holes in it.

"He kissed her on the ___" Most historians believe the blank is lips. He kissed her on the lips. And, at least in one passage, the disciples seemed very jealous of Mary because Jesus obviously trusted her council. The wording almost indicates he is Jesus's favorite among the disciples."

"One of the books left out of the Bible did describe Jesus's childhood, and his supernatural powers were highlighted. For instance, as a child he made clay birds and then called them to live, whereupon, they flew away. Later, he killed another little boy and felt guilty. He brought him back to life. This does not appear in the modern bible."

Bill was now enraptured. Yes, he had known of the lost books purposely left out. He thought there were 7, but maybe more.

"Later, as a child, he disappears, and the Bible does not pick him back up till he is 32 or so. Where did he go? What did he learn? Another Biblical hole. Strangely enough, in Tibet, there is a tale on their prayer wheels of a young man coming from the West to learn of the Tibetan Buddhist teachings. Historically speaking, it was around Jesus's time period. Was that Jesus? Or, maybe an Old One came through to teach Jesus how to control his power and what was his purpose on Earth?"

Bill had never heard this one before.

"I believe he gave an understanding beyond Moses and the Ten Commandments in order to create a higher civilization. He brought God to this planet in a way that many people would believe and follow."

"The Bible is still the most bought book in print. These books are treasured more than any others on Earth. Why? Is it for the beautiful stories, the timeless life lessons? Who knows? But, for certain, Jesus felt the need to help people. I believe there is a lot of truth in the Bible, about what Jesus said and did. His miracles were the Old One's ways. I have seen some of these myself when I was a child, I think. I believe that you have a seed of this power in you! That is until you lost confidence in yourself. Is that what you wanted to hear? None of my words should destroy your faith in the Bible or God. I just question the holes where the answers are lacking."

Again, Tom looked Bill in the eyes.

"Do you understand me?" Tom asked.

Bill seemed to be thinking heavily and came out of it to respond to Tom, "Yes, I believe I do. I truly appreciate all of the time you have spent sharing this information with me."

"But, Tom, since you have these abilities, why have you not put them to use for yourself? You could really be something in this world. You could stand up and be the one people looked up to. You could be somebody." Bill finished.

This time, it would appear that Bill truly had hurt Tom's

feelings. The blush on his cheeks and his suddenly gaping mouth said it all.

He took a few breaths, closed his mouth and regained his composure.

"I guess I don't understand," Tom slowly said, "I guess I do talk too much, cause some of my words meant for your heart and mind, missed their mark. Not everyone in the world is supposed to lead soldiers into battles. Not everyone is supposed to find a cure for cancer. We are not created equal in talents or possibilities or vain pursuits of fame and fortune!"

The last words of 'fame and fortune' was obviously aimed at Bill.

Tom looked away from Bill and said, "We are only created equal in the attempt to do things, some good some bad."

30 – HOW TO RECOVER

Somewhat angrily, Tom said, "Bill, I am right where I need to be, doing what I need to do. This is my life, and I love it. I have the desert, I have Tilley, I have my books. I am something. I think I need to be alone for a bit! I think I will take Sara and Tilley and drive into the desert. Got to think on this! Alone." Tom said.

Then he gained his feet, whistled for Tilley, and the two of them walked out to the truck and left.

His exit left Bill alone and Bill was suddenly overcome with emotions over what just happened.

How could he have been so callous? He had hurt the gentlest man he believed he had ever met. How could he possibly fix what he had broken?

He knew upon Tom's return he had to apologize in the deepest way possible, but this might not be enough.

He began to think it might be more appropriate for him to leave. After all, the highway was not more than an hour's walking distance away. He could warm up his thumb and leave Tom's life as he found it.

Somehow, he knew that was not enough to just leave. Both he and Tom were lost in emotions, leaving the area would just cause them to grow.

So, he began to plan his apology.

31 - APOLOGY AND REJECTION.

Bill spent all day alone waiting for Tom's return and tried every logical twist he could think of to make his apology.

In the meantime, he just felt horrible. He spent a lot of his alone time outside watching nature till way past sundown. Then, he would have a bite to eat and go to sleep on his cot. Eventually, he did, but not without a lot of turning.

Bill woke the next morning to the sound of Tilley whining near his head.

Bill quickly swung his feet to the floor and stood up. Tom must be near, and he wanted to apologize to him right now.

He went outside and found Tom still sitting in the truck.

Bill walked right up to the truck, but Tom held up his hand.

"Nope, you said your peace. I guess I reacted the way I did because it suddenly dawned on me that you were right. After Sheila rejected me, I just wanted to disappear, and this place allowed me to do it. I have been hiding here, as much as living here. I have very few interactions with the outside world. Here, I control all aspects of what I do and what I feel. I have been a coward."

Bill tried, "But, Tom, please..."

"No need. I know you feel bad, but you told me to look in the mirror, and I do not like what I see. I will have to ask you to leave, though. I was so badly hurt by Sheila, and now you. I thought I had recovered, but maybe not!"

Bill stopped looking at Tom in the face and began to scuff the ground with one foot. Man, oh man, he did not want this.

Bill spoke, "You know Tom, I have been a coward as well. I have been hiding from who I was for a long time and trying to keep away from people. Maybe I just projected on you what I saw in myself. How bout this, let me go to the North part of the property and stay there, give you space. Maybe, after a day or two, you might change your mind."

Tom considered that, mulled it over and said, "Ok, that might work. Let me fix you a bedroll and food. Water will not be your problem.

Tom carried out his actions, and Bill walked away to the North.

32 – Reunion

It was 3 days before Tom came to fetch Bill. In the meantime, Bill thought of all kinds of things, still deeply regretting he had hurt Tom.

Tom walked to Bill with Tilley in tow. He extended his hand, Bill shook it, and not one word was said.

The three turned back to the South and walked back to the shack.

A very quiet afternoon ensued.

Tom spoke, breaking the silence, "Bill if you had been me, what would you have done differently? I mean, the Marines was a great experience and I would have not missed meeting Sheila for the world. But, after that?"

Bill was very careful in his response, "Remember Tom, I am just as guilty of hiding away as you are. I lost my very soul. Here, I believe it has come back.
What I want to do is help people now. Maybe, that is what you could have done? Started helping other people."

Tom thought for a minute and said, "Maybe you are right! I should have helped others. I am going to sleep on it!"

Bill woke the next morning to Tom whistling again, in the same toneless way.

Tom looked over at him and said, "You had better get up. I

am running low on food stores. This is probably the last of it till I make a run into Brenda town."

To Bill, Tom was just as friendly and happy as he had been before he had hurt him.

So, the three had breakfast, and Tom talked and passed little jokes, and Bill broke in wherever he could with a retort. It would appear the bad was gone.

Later, all three hopped in Sara and took off for food buying in Brenda town.
This town was located 16 miles East of Quartzite and some 4 miles off I-10. Where they stopped was little more than a convenience store with additional foodstuffs like apples, eggs, and gasoline. But it was very close to the highway, and therefore easy. From everyone's smiles and easy hellos, Bill knew Tom was known and liked.

Bill offered the few dollars he had hidden away to buy stores for the shack, but Tom just waved him off. "Keep it. You might need it later. I have been working these parts for a lot of years. A lot of people will put me to work and pay me."

On the way back, while still on the highway, Bill began to get an idea.

Bill asked, "Tom do you seriously think you should have helped people? And, maybe, you could help other people now?"

Tom looked at Bill while the truck wandered the lanes, "Well Yeah. The more I thought on it, the more it made sense."

Tom looked at Bill's face and asked, "Why do you have that idiotic smile on your face? What in the world are you thinking of?" Tom was a little unsure of Bill's reaction. Bill said nothing, but he had the faintest beginning of a plan.

He looked at Tom, tried the wipe the smile from his face, but it popped back up. So instead, he simply shrugged while pursing his lips together.

Reverend Bill believed he could still save a soul he thought! He might save millions, maybe billions of souls! Just not here on Earth.

He would wait for an Old One to come through the Gate, along with Tom. Meanwhile, he would experiment and practice controlling the outer lying streams of God's Gate. Maybe, by the time an Old One came, he wouldn't have to be taught as much and the Old One would be impressed!

If he could just find an Old One and get them to trust him, he could enter God's Gate. Or maybe they would trust Tom first and Tom could vouch for Bill. Maybe an Old One could help them pick a destination where they could bring the most help.

There he would eventually bring the word of God, interpreted by Reverend Bill, supported by Polecat Tom, to whatever life was out there killing itself. He was not sure how Tilley was rolled into this. But he hoped all three could go together. He had a strong feeling if Tilley could not go, Tom would stay behind as well.

He felt elated!

Reverend Bill said, "Tom, maybe help me help people? You know, the two of us could help people? I bet it would be good for both of us."

Tom snapped his eyes over to him, and asked, "What? What do you have in mind?"

Bill did not look at Tom, but said to Tilley, "It shouldn't be long now."

Tilley just looked at him and wagged her tail slowly, while Tom had to go back to steering Sara between the ditches.

Bill felt he was home now, anyway. He could live here with Polecat and Tilley, given Tom lets him. He could certainly help

Tom around here organizing and cleaning up the place. Maybe, he would start a small garden.

Maybe he should clean up old Polecat and Tilley while he was at it. Get them a bath between the Earth baths. Shine them up, polish them up, maybe haircuts all around.

After all, first impressions are critical, and one's self and disciples reflect one's holy self! He wanted acceptance from an Old One that stepped through the gate for his little family.

He was so excited.

Reverend Bill was back!

Made in the USA
Monee, IL
11 December 2019